# Bedtime Stories for the Criminally Insane

## (and poetry)

by

**Shawn Bailey**

**Thrifty Scribe, LLC**

This book is a work of fiction. Except *Cold Pasta*. Not that I eat dead people's skin, but I have tasted cold pasta, which I truly believe tastes like dead people's skin. And *Changing Stations* actually happened. And I did once win a who-could-eat-the-largest-bug contest by ingesting a rather large grasshopper while drunk, but not a *Firefly*. And unfortunately, A *Murder in the Woods* is based on a true event. Look, who knows what's real anymore? Just pretend it's all as meaningless as your life has been.



Thrifty Scribe, LLC
212 W. Troy St., STE B
Dothan, AL 36303
support@thriftyscribe.com

First Edition, Revised: May 2022
Printed in Dothan, AL US

ISBN 979-8-9859847-0-5

Library of Congress Control Number: 2022906247

Front cover illustration by Marion Rustell Helicame
Back cover illustration by Anna Katorhina
Cover design by Victoria Akinkunmi

1 3 5 7 9 10 8 6 4 2

I don't mean to give you pause; it is simply my nature to do so.

                                              - Comma

Table of Contents

# Introduction

What if every night you went to sleep, there were thousands of spiders at the foot of your bed, and there was nothing you could do about it? Or if you moved into a sentient house that had dementia? Maybe there's a special hospital that can remove your religion as an outpatient surgery, a Christmas tree in a darkened corner of the orphanage that no child would crawl under to get their present, or perhaps there's a scarecrow that bends the boundaries of reality to its will.

In his first horror anthology, Shawn Bailey blends short, horror stories with dark poetry to leave you asking, like the paralyzed victims of the Dancing Scarecrow, what can and cannot be within our fragile realities. The closer you get to the end, the darker it gets.

## Preface

There are many reasons why people don't like poetry.

I think the number one reason is they don't understand what they're reading. Some poetry is vague or has obscure references that, unless you're a medieval renaissance history teacher with a master's in Chemical Engineering, you won't get. Luckily for you, most of my poetry is fourth-grade reading level. But just in case you have trouble, some explanatory notes have been added in the back.

The number two reason people don't like poetry is that they're simple-minded. There. I said it. They want simple sentences that spell everything out with no questions, style, or insight. Thinking about things is hard. So, they just... don't. Well, I can't help you there.

How should one approach poetry? There's a story in one of Howard Stern's books where people are sitting on the floor and eating fried chicken. A guy walks in and, to be funny and gross, pulls his trousers down in front of everyone. One of the guys on the floor reaches over and quickly slides his finger up the guy's ass and back out again, then goes right back to eating his chicken. The embarrassed and violated fellow flees the room. I think good poetry should be like this.

I want you to be going about your day and minding your own business. Then I want to run my creative finger up your literary ass, when you least expect it, and force you to make a decision. Flee now and tell people you've been violated, or grab the hot sauce and wrap your greasy fingers around my poems and stories.

**Nurture**

She never cooked me a
square meal,
but I loved her anyway.

When she stopped breathing yesterday
I carried her gently to
the shed
and lay my tools out
all in order
nice and neat
just like she would have wanted.

I divided her up
evenly and quickly
because she hated it when
I spent all damn day in the shed.

I saved the blood in a pickle jar
in the refrigerator
because she hated it when
I was wasteful.

I spread her in
an even manner
across the backyard
before I tilled it up
because she hated it when
I put all my eggs in one basket.

I put all my tools
right back where they belonged
because she hated it when
I left things lying around.

When the police showed up and
started asking questions
I said I didn't know
because she hated when
I was being a know-it-all.

Spring drifted slowly by.

I watched as the
garden flourished
from a chair
in the backyard
because she said I needed to
get off the couch and
do something.

I weeded the garden
with care
because she hated clutter.

After the first picking
I washed up good
because she said
cleanliness was next to Godliness.

I invited our neighbor
Ms. Jeannie
to share the meal
because she said I should

be more neighborly.

I tried to cook it all
because I needed to be more
helpful around the house,
but Jeannie took over and
finished everything
for me.
I thanked Jeannie
because she said I should
be more thankful
for what I have.

I thanked Jeannie again for a
square meal
but smiled on the inside,
because I knew it came from
my wife's nurturing.

**Will Power**

I am craving a fudge bar
but I shouldn't eat one.

Sooo MANY Calories.

I should have a Popsicle,
and I stare at Lucille Ball
some more
driving away the craving
with bungling, Red Head antics
but a sudden commercial
makes me ravenous
and I wrestle myself
Inside
as I often do
and lose
and get up
and go to the laundry room
and open the floor freezer.

I've put the highest
Calories
under Meighan
where they are much
harder to get,
thinking
my laziness will
prevent my obesity,
but I dig my arm
around under Meighan
until out comes a fudge bar.
It sticks briefly to her

skin, and I pull it free
but she doesn't make
a sound
because I told her not to.

She's an Embryo-shaped
cicle,
all shivery.

There's no head movement
when she looks out the corner
of her eye at me
and I see fear
and I feel guilty
because I know she
is afraid of my
Lack of Will Power.

## Spiders in the Bed

I'm checking for open wounds on my feet so spiders don't crawl inside me during the night. This is not something I worried about this time last year. Spiders weren't always in our beds.

Sure, we had normal house spiders, and some had wood spiders that looked downright nasty. But our beds were usually sanctuary. Tuck those covers under the mattress and you only had to worry about the top parts. All children know that if you hang your hands or arms off the side of the bed, they're fair game for the gremlins and other assorted monsters. But real-world critters we kept at bay by raising our beds off the floor and keeping our laundry fresh and clean. That is, until about a year ago. It all started with the power outage, although calling it that is a bit of an understatement.

The lights didn't just go out in Georgia. They went out for the entire planet. All at once. At 9:38 pm on a Tuesday. No one, even to this day, has a valid explanation of why it happened. It took over a month for the world at large to learn of the disappearance of spiders. After all, how many people take inventory of spiders on a daily basis? There was a study somewhere that said you're probably no further than ten feet from a spider at all times, but they normally keep to themselves. It was the scientists who noticed. Our eight-legged critters vanished from the face of the Earth. They had disappeared overnight, into the void.

At first, it was just the scientists and biologists who were freaking out, while the rest of us wondered what the big deal was if these nasty critters went into hiding. That was fine with us. But as the mystery deepened, the concern started etching its way into other circles. There was a video online where some cameras in a lab in Columbia were recording spiders in their transparent cages. The lights went out, like they did for everybody else in the world, for nine minutes and thirty-eight seconds and when they came back on, the spiders were gone. The thing about this one incident is that these particular spider cages were next to a window and it was daylight out where it happened. So, these black spiders, with yellow patterns on their back, flattened out like someone had squished them between two panes of glass. They rose up from the cage floor and all tilted at the same angle, the same alignment like they were iron filings and someone with a huge magnet was standing over their cages. Then they started rotating, picking up speed with every passing second, until they were spinning like a top. Then they were gone. Just... gone.

We all became amateur spider enthusiasts. Nothing else was talked about for weeks after it picked up in the news. It wasn't, "Did you see the game last night?" It was, "Did you know some spiders can ride their silk like a kite for hundreds of miles?" Or, "Did you know that spiders eat more insects than birds and bats combined?" And it was that last fact that hit home in the summer when crops got hit. Production for wheat, corn, rye, and a smorgasbord of other plants dropped by forty percent. Some countries experienced famine as a result. With no spiders around, it was Insects Gone Wild. Malaria was back in fashion.

We thought things were getting bad, but they got a lot worse. On day 47, there was another blackout. Same time and length as before. The lights came on and people wondered if some other insect disappeared. Scientists took inventory of everything. It didn't take long to figure out what happened, but we're still asking ourselves why. The spiders were back, but only under the covers and at the foot of our beds. You didn't have to go online or ask your neighbors to find out. You could pull back the covers and see for yourself.

My partner and I pulled back the sheets and blankets and peeked under the end of the bed covers. There were hundreds of scurrying little legs undulating at the foot of the bed. We screamed. We got the Raid. We raised the covers enough to create a tunnel to the end of the bed and sprayed enough poison in there to kill an elephant. Then we waited for ten minutes and, being extremely careful, rolled the covers up and took them outside. We hung them over the edge of the deck and shook them. Nothing fell out. So, we laid them on the deck. The covers were soaking wet where we'd sprayed, but not a spider to be found. Not a leg or anything. No trace.

We washed the sheets three times. We went over the bed with a microscope and fine-toothed comb. Found nothing. We cleaned the room. We watched the news. It was happening everywhere. We cleaned the house. Every nook and cranny. I don't even know what a cranny is, but I'm sure we cleaned it. Our house smelled like a factory that produces bleach. We made it to the hardware store just in time to get the last few bags of diatomaceous earth and a few cans of poison.

We returned home and looked at the now naked foot of our bed. No critters. We watched the news again and it wasn't a good thing. There was no choice but to verify what they were saying. After making sure there were absolutely no spiders in our bed or room, we put a sheet over the bed and stood back. In a few seconds, the sheet was moving. We pulled the covers up, this time from the end. Spiders covered the edge. There were so many, we couldn't see the mattress below. We screamed. We stood still and stared. We watched the news again until the wee hours. No way we're going to sleep. The hours that the world slept that night could be counted on one hand.

The horror of what was happening seeped into popular culture. There were documentaries. Horror movies. Songs about it. This was the first mass reporting of a verifiable supernatural event, so you had those end-of-the-world folks coming out of the church's woodwork. And for the first time, a lot of people were listening. They gained traction and a lot of churches started filling up. They weren't locusts, but beggars can't be choosers.

It wasn't long before some brave people started testing out the behavior of our new bedtime visitors. Paid volunteers would get into all types of beds, arranged in assorted configurations. Twin beds, doubles, king-sized, on the floor, raised, spring mattresses, foam, with and without a box spring, with and without sheets, blankets, quilts, and even hammocks and cots. Every combination of everything one can imagine. Here's what they found. The type of bed didn't matter. What mattered were the covers. If you had covers on the bed for more than a few seconds it would draw them out of the void. Take the covers off and they crawled into the bed. Or at least, that's what it looked like. When they cut the beds open, they were nowhere to be seen.

Of course, the obvious was to try and find a workaround. Someone had to. We all had bags under our eyes the size of a Huntsman's egg sac. So far, thousands of people all over the world have died of sleep deprivation. Staying awake for almost a week at a time and dropping like flies. They tried sheets that only went to the ankles, but the spiders appeared on the underside, covering the volunteers' shins. They tried hot sheets and cold sheets. Wet sheets. Covers soaked in bleach and an array of poisons that would kill us before it killed the spiders. No difference in activity. They even tried no beds, just people lying on the cold, hard concrete with covers. In short, if you used covers of any kind, they would show up.

There were exceptions. Some people's beds got infested even without covers. Numerous studies concentrated on what type of people were getting what; down to their DNA. To date, no correlations have been discovered between the people whose beds get infected and those that don't.

Forgot to mention socks. That was the first test that a lot of people did a few days after the event. They had to get some shut-eye. They didn't use covers and crawled into bed in their socks and shoes, just to be safe. As soon as their feet slid down to the foot of the bed, something started tickling the soles of their feet. The spiders were inside their socks. Turns out socks count as covers.

Many resigned to sleeping barefoot with no covers. This was difficult. When you're used to the weight and comfort of covers and you have to go full naked-bed, it's very disconcerting. Add to that the fact that if your bare feet were to edge over the end of the bed, it would sometimes draw a few out. You could feel them crawling across your toes. We screamed and turned on the lights. Nothing. Now, the monsters who come in the night if you let your feet or arms hang over the edge of the bed are real. Tiny, but very, very real.

People didn't wait for scientists to fix things. They experimented themselves. The next trial and error experiments were on predators. Spiders aren't at the top of the food chain. People put frogs, lizards, birds, and even scorpions in their beds. Not sure how a scorpion in my bed is better than a spider in my bed. I would take a bed-full of spiders any day. One guy even used a monkey. Some of them eat spiders, you know. Most of the lizards and smaller reptiles they tried disappeared, one can only assume into that newly created void at the foot of our beds. But the monkey ate his fill of spiders. The next morning, they awoke to a dead monkey. It was lying on its back in the middle of their bedroom floor with its stomach open like someone had thrown an M-80 down its gullet. A splattering of blood droplets on the floor led to the foot of the bed. When they raised the covers, there were five times as many spiders as before, stretching around the sides of the bed.

There were different species of spiders in each bed. Some people had house spiders (the most common) and some had banana spiders. Tiny orbs to giant tarantulas. But every separate bed had the same species. Unless you messed with the ecosystem that is. One person introduced a bunch of Daddy Longlegs into a bed infested with Black Widows. As expected, a bed with Black Widows is more concerning than a bed full of house spiders. Watching over a series of days with flashlights and cameras, they saw the Longlegs dispatch most of the Black Widows. But on day three, they found a thriving population of both spiders, now at opposite sides of the bed.

Everything people tried backfired or didn't work. The only good thing is that our new bedside companions don't seem interested in biting. I mean, if you throw a cricket in there, it's a goner. But many slept barefoot with covers and grew used to it. All but a few never got bit. We couldn't do that. We tried. Having things scurry across your feet is unnatural. As a matter of fact, as one of those documentaries explained, our lizard brain had evolved to see that as a primal kind of threat. So for the first eight months, we slept with no covers and no footwear. Better safe than sorry.

Furniture companies started churning out beds that were a couple of feet longer. That worked half the time. But for half of us, it didn't. Those eight, little hairy legs simply formed a line an inch or two away from people's feet under the covers.

Aside from the psychological effects, one had to be super careful about open wounds. A raw blister on your toe made you free game. You were the monkey. They crawled inside you during the night and laid eggs. scientists said they sprayed some sort of anesthetic on the wound, slipped under the skin, and spilled their progeny into the flesh. If they caught it quick, they might save you. Otherwise... well, like I said, you're the monkey.

So, I check my feet every night. It's amazing what we can learn to live with. We've got a lot of new sects popping up making all manner of promises for cures and poultices to ward off our unwanted companions. Snake oil salesmen around every corner. General angst and foreboding permeate everything. No one fathomed what would come next, but we found out 47 days ago. On the first anniversary of the first blackout. It was at the exact same time as well. Everything went black. When the lights came on, everyone threw covers on their beds and shone their lights to see. The spiders were still there. All our hopes stamped out in an instant.

What then, had disappeared? Turns out China has hundreds of cockroach farms that produce billions of cockroaches every year. They're used as cures for various ailments, but they are also a viable food source for a lot of people. They proliferate like wildfire and have a ton of protein. It's not hard to miss millions of cockroaches when they disappear overnight.

We watched the news like everyone else. In the end, we were too tired and stressed to start trying workarounds that first night. There was an air of resignation as we hit the hay. I asked my partner if they were interested in attending one of those new churches that had popped up down the road, you know, for fellowship and support. They said we might as well. We threw the covers on and bent our knees to keep our bare feet in the center of the bed. The excitement and commotion were under our pillowcases as we laid our heads down for the night.

Tonight, something light and wispy skittered across my feet. The spiders are getting bolder with their nocturnal explorations. Inside my pillow, I hear the crisp wings crackle under the weight of my head, their friction producing a constant notion that the world is beginning to grind itself into oblivion. That things are finally coming to a slow, malignant end. As I somehow begin to fall asleep, I slide my hand, as I've done obliviously all my life, deep into the cavity of my pillowcase. I don't scream. I just pull it out slowly and shake my arm over the edge of the bed.

Turning over on my back, I stare at the ceiling, tears streaming down my face. My mind eventually shuts down and with my racing thoughts subsiding and my tear ducts dry, my eyelids grow heavy. The new visitors vibrate with purpose at the back of my head, and as I drift off to whatever nightmares await, Have I broken the skin on my hands or arms while working in the yard this past week?

**Firefly**

I ate a lightning bug today.

It was dusky and leaves
painted black the purple sky,
and the wind, alas, fainted
from its daily by and by.

The trees with limbs arrest
crossed their branches at their breast
and tapped their roots
with impatient bend
and awaited the Sun
to round again.

As if signaled by the lack of light,
something blinks, in and out of sight.
as my eyes adjust,
shadows glide
flickering yellows
first show, then hide.

Shades a flutter
multiply at will
my open mouth
awaits the kill.

A forward move
my head so quick
and to my tongue
his body sticks.

I chomp and chew
and don't you know
smile ear to ear
with head aglow.

**The Sixth Course**

Fuck me lips
and a Styrofoam face
made for gasoline.

She stutters and spits
like an oilless engine,
groaning and grinding
cunt-like in the neon basement.

From the mouth of God
spews a lava-filled litany
of arcane curses
and forlorn yearning.

Her bruised, steampunk-blue neck
pinned to the soaked mattress
with an afterworld glow
that spreads its glistening tentacles
throughout the concrete room
like gossamer octopi.

The room is pregnant and
screaming pheromones
with piss dribbles of fear.

She is most alive
seconds before her death,
when the swirl of dirty bathwater
draws the last shaved hairs
to the sewer.

-----

She smiles at me from
across the restaurant linens and
asks if we can go back to her place.

First dates are so stressful.

The Headless Horseman,
nauseated
from a night of revelry,
leaned over his toilet
and...
did nothing.

**High Tide**

We laughed and played and laughed
As the waves broke on the shore
And the Sun baked the sand
And the children screamed for more

Seagulls clustered here and there
Awaiting special treats
We played until our skin burned red
And sand crept into our seats

Then the growing ball of Orange
Slightly touched the ocean
Testing the water first,
It seemed to cease its motion

"Time to go," I yelled and
shoulders slumped in sorrow
"No fussing or complaining
And we might come back tomorrow."

Then the children smiled
A new light in their eyes
"We have something to show you.
It's a really big surprise!"

They know I love surprises
As I follow them to the spot
Where they've dug a rather large hole
For such a tiny tot

C'mon dad they beg
We'll do it really quick

So I climb into the hole
That they've hollowed with a stick

They pushed the sand around me
I played along with a giggle
Until the sand was packed so tight
That I could hardly wiggle.

One last tip of Orange
Cast a faint glow to their faces
And they smiled even wider
As they ran back to their places

They laughed and played and laughed
As the waves broke on the shore
And I screamed until I couldn't
My throat raw, and sore

I looked up at the Moon
Brilliant in the sky
And couldn't move my arms
Though I try and try and try

I cried until I laughed
Then I laughed until I cried
Then I smiled to myself
And giggled by and by

Hours came and went
And boredom took its toll
Monotony crept upon me
In my sandy little hole
I laughed and laughed and laughed
As the waves broke on the shore

Then I laughed and laughed and gurgled
And then I laughed no more.
So when it's time to leave,
And they wanna stay and play
Don't put off 'til tomorrow
What can be done today.

# A Murder in the Woods

We were deep in the woods. Not like you see in the movies, but a couple of miles nonetheless. Here's the way it works - the foreman sits in his air-conditioned truck and points across the deep, rolling hills, about a half mile away. *I'll pick you up on the other side*, he says, and drives away. He makes about seventeen dollars an hour, which is about double what I make, and does it without breaking a sweat. Sure, he worked at this bullshit for years before he got where he's at, and probably deserves to sit in that cool-ass truck, but when it's 102 degrees outside, that doesn't really count for shit.

I stand in the middle of the dirt road, following the power lines with my eyes, up and over the mountains. There's a forest to one side, then fifty or sixty feet of relatively open space, and then a forest on the other side. I say "relatively open", because mother nature's been doing her thing for a few years without being checked. That's my job today, and for that matter, every day, Monday through Friday. I put on my heavy chaps. It's like wearing a coat on your legs, but it beats missing chunks of your thighs if the saw kicks back. I shredded a part of mine last month; tired in the heat and being lazy. So I wear mine. I pick up two-and-a-half gallons of gas in one hand and my chainsaw in the other. I walk to the edge, gas up, and start clipping the smaller trees and bushes, zig-zagging back and forth between the middle of the power line's path and the left side of the forest line. It's 6:15 in the morning, already 80 degrees. I'm sweating like a stuck pig only five minutes into the day.

Around noon, my neck starts stinging from the sweat and won't stop. I finally figure out it's not sweat, but wasps. I drop my chainsaw and run up the hill. The others sling gas at them. One fellow finally retrieves it for me. I've been stung about ten or fifteen times. We take a break. The guy who drives the tractor sets his can of beans on the idling engine for an exact amount of time and opens the perfectly heated can. Then it's back at it. It's over 100 degrees and humid when we stop for the day. We take apart our chainsaws and clean them with air pressure and gas, a stupid Friday ritual that leaves me with heartburn for the weekend. Before we go, I have to crap, so I head off up the road with toilet paper in hand. No porta-potties out here.

They're back at the truck waiting. The woods are open, so I walk about 75 yards over a rise. No downed logs to sit on, so I hold a small tree trunk to keep my balance and do my thing. On my way back I hear a muffled squeal just off the path. I walk about twenty feet and see the poor thing immediately. It's a puppy. Someone's dropped it off in the woods, like that's giving it a goddamn chance or something. Like it can find its way home like in the movies. It's about four months old at best, and I can see immediately that there's no saving it. It has a wound of some sort on its side, above its back leg, and it's teeming with maggots. Inside and out.

I think about how to clean it out, kill all those nasty bastards eating him alive. Maybe I can pour gas on it and - no, I already hear the howls. He's breathing heavy; his energy gone. It's like he already knows. I can't put him in the truck with maggots everywhere. I can't kill the maggots inside of him without harming him as well. There's no saving him. I'm young, so I get one of the older guys from the truck and show it to him. He curses and tells me there's nothing that can be done. I ask if we have a gun in the truck. We do not. We have an axe.

I walk back and get the axe. The trek back to the dog is a blur. I think of my wife and kids playing in the yard at home. An uncle's funeral. A downed power line I saw earlier by the river. Was it live, lying there in a puddle of rainwater? My dog at home. Where I will strike? How hard you have to swing an axe to kill a puppy on the first blow? In my mind, I see some asshole in a pickup tossing his puppy onto the dirt road and driving off. I throw my axe at the back of his pickup and it smashes through his window, cleaving his head into. He runs off the side of the mountain and his mangled truck burst into flames.

I ride back to the drop point with five other guys. They joke and carry on. Farting and rolling up the windows. As if everything is as it should be.

When I get home, Charlie is waiting for me, turning circles and nibbling my beard when I lean down for kisses. I wash. I eat. As we prepare for bedtime, I go into the kitchen and open a new pack of bologna, pulling the little, red plastic rings from each piece. He eats them one by one. Charlie is happy. I am happy.

I lie awake until three in the morning thinking about why we clean and sharpen our chainsaws every Friday, but never sharpen the axe.

## Stereotypes

I squirm into position
cheeks evenly distributed
pasted gently to white plastic
my twirly tucked and aimed
feet planted on the cold green tile.

Down to my right
next to a trickle of leaking water
is a cockroach.
I call him Jervis
as he has no discernable method
to relay his name.
He lie upon his winged back
a silent witness to my solitary ritual.
Having little in common
I remain silent,
awkward tension waxing.
I cannot perform my… duties.
"How is the foraging?"
*Idiot.*
Roaches don't forage, do they?
Scavenge perhaps, but what a dirty-sounding word.
It was out there.
Too late to apologize.
Silence.
I did not intend offense,
to categorize
to stereotype.
I have friends that are roaches.
Perhaps he is sleeping.
*Idiot.*
Roaches don't sleep, do they?

Like sharks?
Perhaps a submissive gesture then?
After all, I am the Alpha male.
I reach down to tickle Jervis
on the belly, thorax, what have you,
and his left leg twitches in protest.
I have been presumptuous, assuming.
I retract, stare forward.
I was only trying to be friendly.
"Are you injured, sir?" I yell,
self-conscious of my own ire.
"Excuse me?" he retorts.
I am shocked, recalcitrant.
The person in the next stall leaves abruptly.
I do not believe they cleaned themselves.
It was not Jervis who spoke.
My embarrassment is acute,
like the pains in my abdomen.
I stand quickly.
"GOOD DAY TO YOU, SIR!" I scream,
and leave.


Some stereotypes are true, I suppose.
Goddamn roaches.

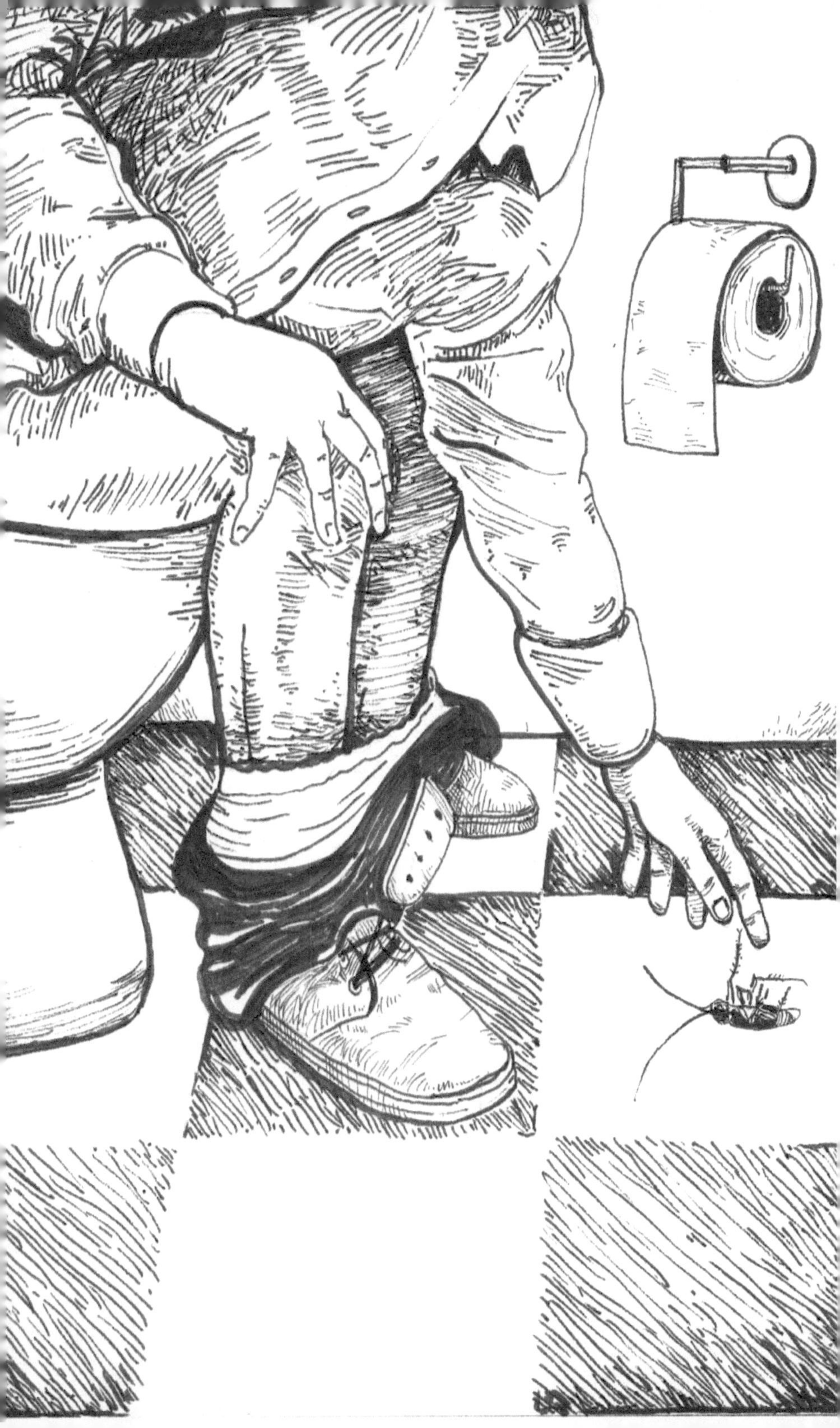

**The Last Anything**


I pass by the 2 percent milk
and see a lonely carton of grey,
sunken back against a
cold, aluminum cavern.


It must be sad for the eggs
that no one even bothers to peek inside
and see for sure if anything is
wrong with them.


And as they huddle for warmth
in the dairy florescence,
I stroll past and walk
the linoleum isles


alone

**Fishing with Walter**

I watched the plane pitch sideways
from the stern of my boat
and he spilled out the door
like a clumsy anecdote.

It rained down a Walter
that lovely afternoon
who when he met the lake
popped like a balloon.

The water's surface tension
made for a wall
And did a very poor job
of breaking Walter's fall.

But the plane didn't crash
and righted and then flew
on to Syracuse,
New Delhi and Peru.

All that's left of Walter
who is with this world no more
is a flattened sense of being
and a ripple on the shore.

I reel my line back in
and row bleakly for the bank
and try to remember where
poor old Walter sank.

But they never found old Walter
and doubted me they did
another fishing story
from this old man they bid.


---


I'll always wonder why
that plane spit Walter out
and left him wet and soggy
and swimming with the trout.

So you'll understand then
why it shook me to the core
and why me and jet airliners
have an ominous rapport.

Every time we shake a little
or turbulence we hit
I scream out Walter's name
and take a soggy shit.

**Baptist Outpatient**

I had my Religion out this morning.

These days it's an outpatient,
not like ages ago when the king himself
had to forcibly remove it.

I couldn't go to church for six months prior,
couldn't quote the bible until I'd read the whole thing,
had to read *Handmaid's Tale* and not root for the Commander,
had to agree that thoughts and prayers
can't stop bullets or viruses,
couldn't say things happen for a reason
without mentioning cause and effect,
had to sign a disclaimer that I understood
I would no longer be seriously considered
for political positions,
had to understand that *all lives* include *black lives*
and that no one in the bible was white
and read about the Nicene creed,
and that if Jesus is God then he committed suicide,
couldn't dress nice on Sundays
unless I also dressed nice through the week,
couldn't give glib responses to complex questions
while donning an all-knowing smile,
had to pick a random foreigner and
start a conversation with them,
had to read the classics,
Plato, Aristotle, Socrates,
and for some reason
even though I was getting my religion out
I had to read books on *other* religions,
had to read Hitchens, articles on Westboro Baptist,

magazines on war in the Middle East,
*lots* of reading for some reason,
couldn't watch Lifetime and had to watch R-rated movies
with dirty words and sex scenes with unmarried people,
had to cut out country music,
couldn't participate in any function that contained
interpretive dance,
had to exclaim, 'No fucking way!'
in a crowded restaurant loud enough for people to overhear,
had to read the *Declaration of Causes of Seceding States,*
to know that toxic masculinity isn't the same as masculinity
had to watch all the Harry Potter films,
utter the phrase, 'Protego' at myself in a mirror
then shake uncontrollably while pretending to have
caused an infinite paradox,
could not tuck my shirt in,
had to watch more than one news channel,

And I had to do all this before they would even consider
taking it out.

They said while they were in there they went ahead and
removed what they could of my Guilt.

But I know they didn't get it all
because I sometimes feel like I did a bad thing
by having it out.

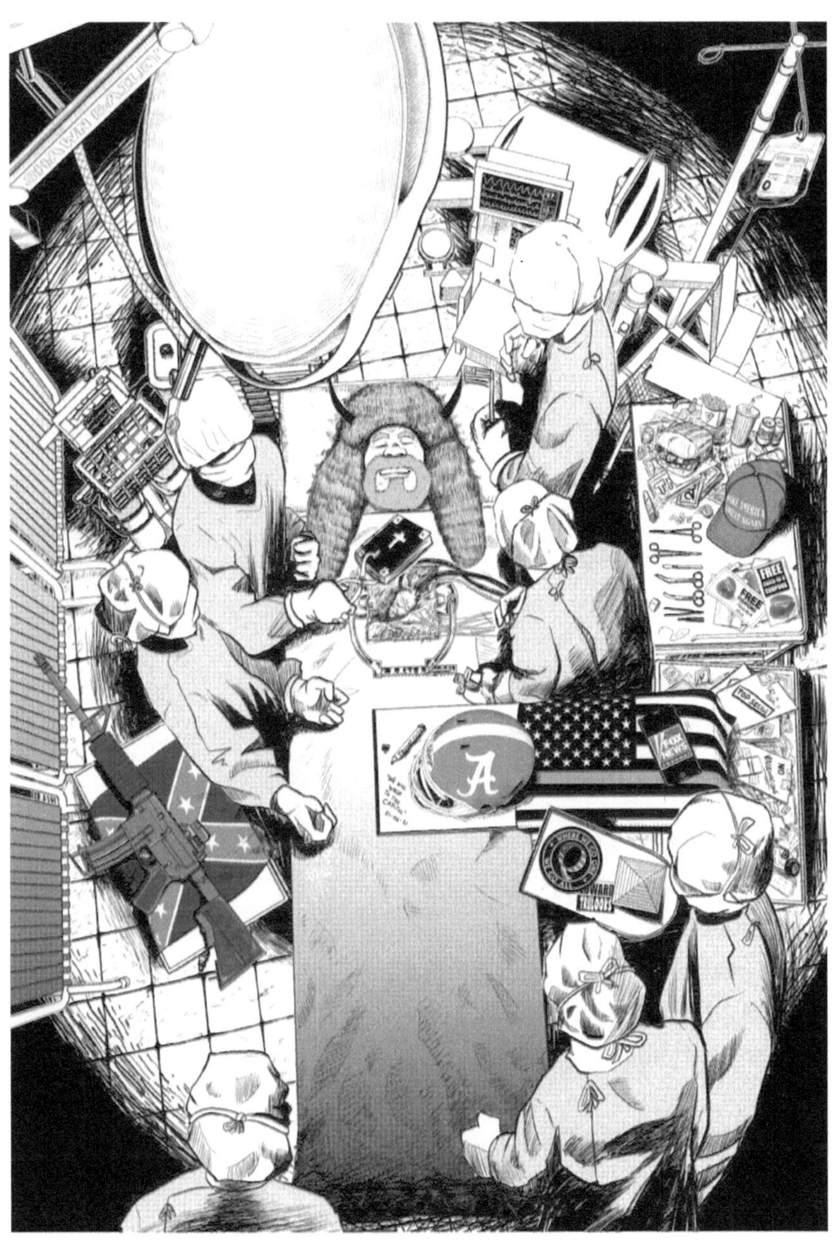

**Scientific Inertia**

Mr. Bachenstein was quite fine
walking home from work,
a light stroll until he suddenly
flew into the air and sped like a rocket
head first
into the bottom of a dangling piano
nine floors above.

And birds, well… they just had to
learn to eventually fly upside down
and build their nests on the underside of the branches.

And fish, well… they rode the largest
blue flying amoeba ever to the exosphere
where the oceans splashed against nothingness
and formed a blurry prismatic shell for those of us
clinging to lamp posts and
clustered, confused on ceilings.

And Remi and Ted's Pinto
lifted off like at the end of Grease
but they weren't singing,
just screaming for some long minutes
until, as they suffocated slowly,
they saw a tidal wave coming to swallow them whole.

And so with differentiation at work again
we're all finding it hard to breath
and so if you find this note in a bottle years from now
know this: it was dropped by a scientist from the doorway
of a lab in Switzerland into the seas above
and we found the Higg's boson

and we are sorry about the Gravity thing.
In our defense, it was an outlier, you know.


49

**Thing Could Be Worse**

They say things could be worse
and of course, they're right
things could be worse
if ticks took to flight.

Falling from pine trees
not counted in
these beasts are grounded
save a big gust of wind.

But if wings did sprout
translucent with veins
on these eight-legged
swells of arachnid strains
they would doubtless
cause a panic sour
about the size
of the Eiffel Tower.

We would shun bugs
like roaches and cease
to care about spiders
in the very least.

And the thousands of eggs
once laid on the ground
would spread far and wide
as they flew all around.

Legions, they would come
digging into skin
and you couldn't really

tell where or when
until they bloated and
off they were lopped
or just over-ate, swelled,
and popped.

And forget lollygagging
on a bright sunny day
or strolling to the park
to dance around and play
cause the sun's blotted out
and you can't see a thing
for the Dermacentor Andorsoni
and the I. Ricinus string.

Barber shops would profit
from head overhauls
it's easier to see ticks
when your head's completely bald
and since you never know
where they might roam
some of the shaving you'd
have to save for home.

Outdoor pets would be
all out of luck
so we'd move indoors
all the moos and the clucks
and dogs and cats
would have to coexist
and things would all smell
like animal piss
and that's no good
'cause you can't get a date

wearing yellow No. 5
from a goat named Kate.

No more picnics
lying next to the waves,
rollercoasters
or Atlanta Braves.
No Monday Night Football
concerts in the park
something scuttling
creepy, in the dark.

So when they mumble clichés
like "things could be worse"
say "yeah, ticks could fly,
and suck us 'til they burst."

**Rut**

Thirty-four
and in the same town
I grew up in,
a stagnant sea of tradition
inside a Baptist Box.

This syrupy mindset
begins with lazy trips
from the couchtv to the microwave
from the shower to the job
from the couchtvmicrowave to the bed.

I productionline a samepath existence
and don't notice I'm sinking
into a samepath rut.
My smalltown thinkshoes are sinkheavy
in the mindlessmudruts.
Back and forth
Back and forth
Back and forth
And suddenly I'm in the
basementmold of a samethinkcorridor
looking up for light
and there is none.

I bump into oldhighschooldrinkingbuddies
in the dark
and they are the same as the day I left them,
like someone yelled *freeze* and forgot to yell *unfreeze*
and they are all glibhappy in their blindness.

And suddenly I want out
but I'm middleearthdeep and futureblind.
I slowclaw my way to the surface
and now I can't bring myself to peer
back down into that samepathchasm
that is nothing more than my past self.

I tiptoe across this fragile Earth
watching for those brash, uninformed corridors
filled with
apathy
narcissism
ignorance
racism
fear
religion
ready to swallow my verve whole
and set like concrete around my multicolored feet.

**Shiny Happy People**

The mirror spilled liquid
onto the floor
my vanity leaking
into a polished mercury pool
of turbulent diffraction.

I shoveled the warbly sludge
into the bathtub
and rooted in its chrome
like a reflective boar.

Shiny molecules filling
every cavity
scrubbing away my narcissism,
replacing illusions
with a fine, metallic certainty.

I was a glut of silver
cycling to work
and causing wrecks
with intimate, sidewalk distortions.

At work, Stanley followed
me around
staring and smiling
so wide I could see
all thirty-two teeth.

The others talked briefly
then turned away
from themselves,
from me.

Lonely, I stared into
the bathroom mirror,
into infinity
and was unable to properly
reflect on myself.

I felt uncomfortable
in my own skin
and so peeled it off
and reveled in my insecurity.

**Boards and Nails**

Me and Lanie
are soooo creative.

We are playing
the nails in the board game
on County Road 107
but everybody 'round here calls it Bynum Leatherwood.

The summer asphalt is
baking my skin
right through the back of my shirt
but we giggle through the pain
peering over the hill
waiting.

I am the board
and she is the nails
so she gets to lay on top of me
squishing the breath out of me
and wouldn't you know,
right before it's my turn
to be the nails
a big ole truck comes flying over the hill.

The joke's on the lady
gabbin' into her cell phone
'cause she don't see the
board with the nails in it,
giggling in the road.

OUNTY ROAD
107

## Ego

I am a raging poet,
my inked hatchet
flesh-wedging a spray of bloody
word foam onto the triage
of paper,
bending
folding
spindling
mutilating
a torrent of liquid emotion,
wrenched thought spasms
corrugated prisms of mind swell,
and when I have wrought and reaped,
stretched my filigree soul over
a brittle weave of yellowed paper,
soaked the pages with philosophical blood,
crimson views of humanity, caramelizing
the sticky pages together,
a pungent weld of glory and desperation,
my wife looks it over and says,
"Yeah, cool."

**Dancing Scarecrows**

The Scarecrows dance and
the Scarecrows twist
an age-old jig known only to them,
and with a jubilant thrust
and a flick of the wrist
wave their crispy arms skyward
made of corn husk and limb.

They merrily sneak from hither and thither
and play hide and seek with Old Man Winter.

Their burlap mouths
stitched carelessly so
speak a fluent dialect -
the language of Crow.

They conversate with crows
explaining away,
and apologizing for,
what they do every day.

Then they all come together
in the center of the field
and talk of old times
with a Yuletide zeal.

The snowflakes gently drift
amidst the dried and jagged stalks
and with the reaping far behind
they hold their Scarecrow talks.

When they hear the farmer's truck
approaching with a clatter
the December soil
crunches as they scatter.

The farmer looks across his field
and smiles with country charm
at the Scarecrow, Christlike,
with a crow upon its arm.

**The Clock**

My troubles all started 15 minutes ago
when the clock ticked a stop and ran really slow.

All the people I loved who didn't love me back
all seems now, rather matter-of-fact.
The luxurious items I could not afford
all the cars I drove that I did so adore.
But the gold and the jackets estate sales did claim
and the Porsche and the Lexus are all but a name.
And the plasma I watched from the living room wall
and the front load washer standing seven feet tall
are in someone else's house or in someone else's hall.
The trophy wife I landed with my TV and my car
Is reading life insurance papers at the local bar.
The estate in which I lived, with movie room and pool
was my kingdom here on Earth which I can no longer rule.
And as I float above my body and the surgeon tries his best
there is one last thing that I really must confess.
I've had it all wrong from the very, very start
for all these things I mention lie nowhere near the heart.
As they call the time of death I take a moment to reflect
and see my life, like my car, was a crumple of a wreck.
I made myself an island, accomplished well and spent
credit cards galore, and loved every cent.
But it's people I have missed, that necessary part
more precious than the original, Italian works of art.
Some people take with them the heartache and the sorrows
from the loved ones and the kin who weep for all their
morrows.
And dreary though it is this brokenness, a gift
we can carry with us here, far and wide across the rift.
But today no one weeps, no tears for me to keep

as I travel my last path through the far and wide and deep.
I didn't see my time here as painful until now
I wish to set things straight, but cannot figure how.

So I say these words to you, embrace well others there
and for material things, do not give a care.
For at some point in time, which you will not know
the clock will tick a stop and run really slow.

**Cupid's Rusted**

They are waiting on the
Other side, like they have
since the day you were borne.
Your cocoon of bedsheets
holds your essence at bay
and your blank stare
leaves only windows

Opaque.

You sit with the Sandman
and he speaks; his words
made of dreams
bathed in memories,
parted by a decaying mind
whose nights and days are

One.

A cascade of doors open
but you see only yours
and as the hinge creaks
you realize you are not

Ready.

Amongst the Calling of Souls
cries a whisper
and the Tally ceases at the

Threshold.

A synapse of pain
spirals down through
a conical vortex of
withering turbulence and
explodes at the
Event Horizon.
You have sealed your
Gateway with
Sinews of Sorrow
Weakness of Will
and a single speck
of skin, bat of an eye
and wrinkle of nose.
A careless smile was
used to pierce the flesh,
a gauntlet of soft words
to paralyze the will,
a demeanor like velvet
to puncture the heart.
But that which bore
the cave, that which
ground the abyss of
emptiness and desolate
caverns within your soul,
you know not of its

Origin.

It was cloaked in a
Sea of Veiled Perception.
You fell to blindness and
ran towards the darkness,
reveled in its blackness,
bathed in the lack of hope

it produced, and happily allowed the
frigid waters of ignorance to
fill your lungs as you
drowned willingly and (seemingly)
of your own hand.
But that hand was not
your own, and with
this dealer, the house always wins.
That which can only be given
was at the same time taken,
wrenched from the whole
ferried across the purgatory
of anticipation and
False Hope only to be
denied of possession by
the very thief who lifted it.
That part of your soul
lies now outside of you
in the Void,

Lost.

It is tethered still by an
umbilical of passion that
will never cease,
never die,
never rest.
Unaware is the one who
holds sway, the one who
trails your sliver of soul about
like a blind doe clutching
her mother's tail.
The tornado's eye
sees only calm

and nothing of the
twisted ruin dealt by its

Path.

This peaceless circle
of your highs and lows
sits atop your head
and spins,
Incessantly.
You wish to pass whole
but that portion is

Forsaken.

You are pulled through
the Gate of your own making,
sideways and screaming
and the sliver catches on
the Door.
It is pain.
It is not permeable to
this World.

Cupid kneels and with
a black, rusted bucket,
he catches the sliver as
it snaps and drops, then
dips a barbed arrow into
the never-ending poisons of

Lost Dreams.

**Hello, Friend**

"Hello, friend"
said the cipher mundane
An obsidian enigma
dressed in clothes very plain

"I'm numbers and letters
nothing more, A to Zed."
"Oh... Cool,"
I believe is what I said.

We performed a secret handshake
and agreed on protocol
but when asked for secret phrases
I knew not one at all.

The cipher began to walk away
and leave me all alone
all because my desk got cleaned
and sticky notes were gone.

I began to scream and yell,
pitched a fit, flailed my arms
but the cipher in plain clothes
was immune to all my charms.

My blood began to boil
my face grew crimson veins
until one burst at last
spraying scarlet my domain.

I collapsed onto my desk
And drug it to the floor
as my head bounced on the carpet
I began to be no more.

As the light drained from my eyes
and the world began to dim
a yellow square I noticed
as my soul hung from a limb.
They had spilled out from a drawer...
"password1" I whispered meek
but the cipher whispered back
"that sounds a little weak."

**Green Thumb**

Grandma was such
an adept gardener,
no one let her
bury the dead.

## ELO

I spin into the void

My link broken
to the mothership

Five hours of air
if I'm lucky


I twist at the event horizon

A helpless crew
watching the me-dot

for a bag of tricks
that will not come


I rotate and deform

Can feel the Hawking Radiation
mumbling to my dark matter

body wrenched and convoluting,
writhing in space-time

I gyrate and change shape

minutes turn to hours,
years . . . eons

I poke a hole in my tank,
set myself ablaze with my welder

I hear ELO's *Fire on High*

and sing the intro
for eternity

swelling until I am the size of everything,
an infinite, dilating pirouette

## Behavioral Psychology of Woodpeckers

We both have deadlines
he and me and
we're not so different really
except he bangs his head against his desk
like a ravenous djinn gone mad inside
his emerald coated bottle of a cubicle
and he does this for three minutes
and then a small hole forms
just an eggshell patina break
and he uses his teeth to snag
some object in it...

Paper!

A wadded, rolled up, already stapled and collated
report for the boss
and I just stare at him and then
I stare at my monitor as he
pulls it ex nihilo from the mini fissure
in his desk.

Everyone skips to lunch and
I'm alone and
behind and
worried and
so I bang my head
like he did
really, really hard
but can't make three minutes' worth
and then I wake up on a nightly vacuumed carpet
and see a circle of eyes peering down
and feel crimson running from my forehead

and I think
just like a Robin
that a Woodpecker
is just a crazy bird.

**Changing Stations**

There's a guy in the car next to us
surfing the stations
and I decide to surf mine.
I press four buttons and skip
the missing one
and then hit SCAN.


I look up
at a green light and take my foot
off the brake
moving it quickly to the gas.
I need to move fast today because
I am behind on everything.
Money.
Gas.
Loose belts.
Novel editing.
Kickstarter T's.
January's rent payment.
Stores that carry '92 Nissan pickup belts.
So I have to move fast because life is a race
and it's so easy to finish the race
with nothing accomplished
and your children following in your footsteps.
I'm turning left to go to Wal-Mart
before heading to Governor's where they carry the A\C belt
because I have to get                                    .



GLASSMETALCRUNCHINGPAIN.

Not mine, but I can feel it.
I turn to my wife who is 'Oh my Godding' and
tell her to "come sit where I am and get our car out of the
road."
Someone is dead.
Of that I am sure.
A tan SUV never hit the brakes
and so it flipped and landed
uncatlike on its side while the guy in the TBone
is angled down into the culvert
and is sliding, with much less blood than one would imagine,
out of his crumpled door like a lazy fried egg,
thrashing in pain as if covered in ants and blind
and holding his chest and looking nowhere.

I look over at the SUV and a colorful fat lady is climbing out
through the windshield.

People come from all sides to the huddle,
a few calling plays –
turn his car off
don't move, don't let him move
Memorial and __________, and yes it's bad!  We need an
ambulance now!

My wife leans over and stops him from moving,
talks to him
tells him what happens
each time he asks,
gives him a focal point.
He stops moving around
and I see blood in his eye
as I look for embedded glass
and lean in his car to find the radio is still playing.

I turn the car off and
lean into the door, scrunching it back against metal
so it won't open on the guy.
His wallet is under him and
I pick it up and hold it, with his keys,
and give them to a busy paramedic.

I look over at the fat lady and chubbyyounggirl standing in the
median.

They are dressed from one of those stores that rich men's
wives open in strip centers because they're bored.
The kind that sell gaudy blandishments for ridiculous prices.
The girl jumps straight up and down and whines for her daddy.
Neither plump is visibly hurt.
Neither plump has walked over to check on the man in limbo.

I wonder if she was on the phone and
have a sudden urge to grab her
by her fatblondehead and drag her across glassmetal
punching her in the face along the way
over to the man whose life/song she interrupted
and make her –

"Can you drive a stick shift?"

A strange question in the now.
A lady left her truck in the turning lane.
A five speed.
I make my way across four lanes
*very carefully*
and move it,
then
*very carefully*

back
then
I am
handing over a stranger's keys for the second time this day.

I want to remember the song that was playing on his radio,
and on mine.
so I can cross reference them and pour my metaphysics
into them when I think of
paths and milliseconds and God.

**Cold Pasta**

*How does dead skin taste?*
I repeated back
laughter muffled
like the smothered homeless
to officer shiny pants.
His partner, vomit-ridden
with us both
for illusory discrepancies
crimes against humanity
omnivorous and blatant
on the green porcelain plate.
*Like cold rigatoni*
I said
and it turned out to be
too simple a metaphor,
too easily grasped
and the shiny pants smile
quizzical, indifferent, numb

transmogrified

because now...
now
now
they tasted that rigor mortis pasta
like I did.

And just like that
significant others will wonder
what's wrong with their simple Italian dishes.

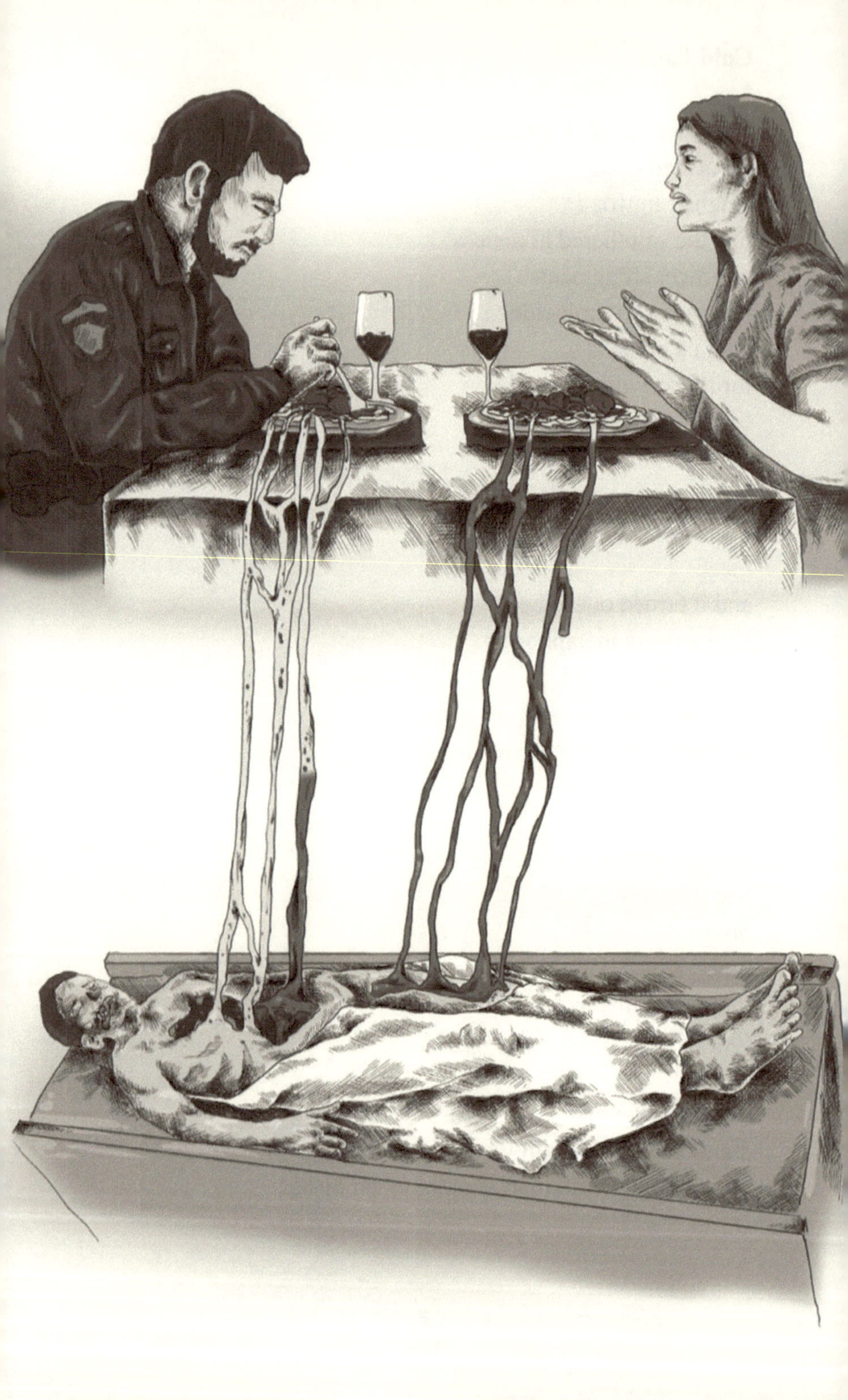

**Unspoken**

When I was living
I left fear voids,
an embarrassed unspeaker of things that
should be said,
comforting things,
cool bed covers on a summer's day things.
Each well-thought-out novel excerpt
bottled up into an awkward moment's
silent little soliloquy.

Each repressed emotion
too cliché,
too much like a movie line,
rehearsed sounding,
as if mumbled sideways by some sappy poet,
ready to expose my delicate ego
to some mirage of infinite possible responses,
or worse,
left desolate in wide open silence.

It was these Unspoken things
that were swallowed by swift moments,
hesitations led by a tug-boat of doubt,
slow moving but of powerful persuasion
tightening the unsure rope around the words
on the tip
of
my
tongue
and dragging them to the back of my
remorseful throat.
And the dead drew tears.

They would never know the words
I had kept to myself.

Then I died
and went to a place
similar to what you'd think
and they sat me gently down
at a wooden desk and slid a book under my nose.

The title was simple:
Unspoken.

The authors were many
and line one, chapter one read
"I'm sorry.  I didn't mean that."

And the living drew tears.

# I

I am standing naked on a
smooth, round Earth.
There is nothing here but me.
No objects and no people.
I am tired, so I look and see a chair
is behind me.
I sit.

# II

I am young and time passes
slowly and there is
nothing to do.
I am bored.
I get old and then
I die.
What was the point of all that?

I am young and time passes
slowly and there is
a ball in front of me
RED
against all this whiteness
and I think that's neat.
I play with the ball and
it bounces and bounces and it is
sometimes hard to catch.
Years pass and
I am bored.
I get old and then
I die.
What was the point of all that?

I am young and time passes
slowly and there is
nothing to do.
There is nothing here but me.
No objects and no people.
I am tired, so I look and see a chair
is behind me.
I sit.
There is a noise to my left
and I look to see a PERSON
We are a little nervous,
two people in two chairs and
no other people anywhere and
what in this glassy white world is
there to say?
But we speak
We get to know each other
and have long talks and
smile sometimes and
when we get older we find
a bouncy red ball and
laugh together at the fact that just
bouncing it back and forth to each other is
so much fun.
Years pass and
we get old and then
we die.
A sad ending, but… worth it.

I am young and time passes
slowly and there is
nothing to do.
I look down and there is GREEN grass
beneath my toes.
I wiggle my toes and smile and
look behind me and there is a small hut.
Water starts to hit the top of my head and
it is cold so I step into the hut and look back out
and marvel at the water as it
leaks slowly from the grass onto the
Earth's white surface.
There is a door, a window, and a bed in my hut.
I am happy to lie down and rest in my VERY OWN hut.
Years pass and I walk out of my hut and there is a large
HOUSE sitting just a red ball's throw away.
It is the size of twenty of my huts.
It has grass also but it looks a little…
greener.
And there is a large, majestic gate
surrounding it and there are tons of RED balls
on the grass.
Some red balls are very LARGE.
I walk over to the gate and press a GOLD BUTTON
and I am excited to hear another person's voice.
"Yes?"
They are nervous like me but that's ok.
"Hi, would you like to play ball?"
I am smiling.
"NO," they say. "I don't know you. Please go away."
Now water is falling from my head as I
go back to my LITTLE hut.
I grow old and bored and I can only
look at all the other balls in the green, green yard

with the mean gatekeeper.
I am lonely and angry and mad and so I
throw my red ball at a window in the big house
and it breaks and I am scared but happy as I
run back to my hut.
No one ever comes out.
Years pass and
I am bored.
I get old and then
I die.
What was the point of all that time
I had to spend not getting the things I wanted?

I am young and time passes
slowly and there is
nothing to do.
I look down and there is GREEN grass
beneath my toes.
I wiggle my toes and smile and
look behind me and there is a LARGE HOUSE.
I walk across the most wonderfully colored grass
to my VERY OWN house and smile and fall asleep
on the softest bed ever.
When I awake, I look out my window and there is
a small little hut across the way.
I am worried at what kind of creature could
live in a hut that small.
It could come out and take one of my balls from
the grass and so now there is a large gate
wrapping around my house.
And a good thing too because sure enough
someone has come from that small little hut
and is trying to get at my grass and red balls and
maybe they even want to come and take my
house away.
They walk over to MY gate and press MY GOLD BUTTON
and I can hear a crazed excitement in their voice.
"Yes?"
I am nervous because I do not know if they
can get in.
"Hi, would you like to play ball?"
I am frowning
and I knew they wanted to take my red balls
from MY grassy yard.
"NO," I say. "I don't know you. Please go away."
Now I cannot leave my house
or they will come in and take my things

and so I am trapped here forever.
Years pass and
I am bored.
I get old and then
I die.
What was the point of all that time
I had to spend trapped in my house?

# III

I am standing naked on a
smooth, round Earth.
There is nothing here but me.
No objects and no people.
I am tired, so I look and see a chair
is behind me.
I sit.
Anything can happen now
I guess.

**Buttercream**

I came home at 8:15
and locked my door.

I set my custom alarm and
set things in motion,
as I always do
on full moons
once a month.

And the lights flash on
and light floods the room
and all my friends from work
are smiling and holding gifts
and there is a beautiful cake
on the table.

I feel guilty as the
Full Moon
washes over me like a
nocturnal, silver soul
and my friends scream and scream,
but I've got bars on the windows and
soundproof walls
and as my
canines
expand fast enough to crack my jawbone,
I wonder what kind of icing is on the
Cake?

**Preposthumous Poet**

Whereas I am hereby acknowledging my inclination to excel
in any and all profitable prose, or in a manner poetry, verse,
short story and up to and including anything with alphabetical
value, I do hereby propose to solicit the general public, not
excluding anyone specifically, for that which I hold most dear
amongst all my endeavors.

Before my modest proposal, no pun intended, is most
generously offered to scribes and the common man alike,
inclusive to the illiterate and poverty stricken who retain
charitable donations or able of self to pay in kind, I would
offer an explanation considering a dilemma that has sought to
plague the gifted, the verbally endowed, and creative beings of
most noble a nature.

A vicious conspiracy, whose origin has been at the center of
much debate, has infested not only the Earthen cultures
perceived by man in accordance with his five trusted senses,
but has reached beyond the grave itself into the very pit of Hell
and the furthest leagues of the Empyrean. It is of a grave
nature, no pun intended, that afflicts mostly the dearly
departed, who by the nature of their subterranean
imprisonment, can n'er raise the sharpened points of their pens
to strike back against the beast whose mouth froths the last
poisonous irony, and whose gut digests the whole of laughter
and tears, not to mention gold and coin, that would have been
to the liking of the aforesaid at a much earlier and convenient
time.

The evil I speak of is Praise. An exaltation of poets and the
like only available posthumously and too often a few turns of
the century in the making. Every worthy scholar who has

yielded great enough good fortune to succumb to its literary
necessity can vouch for the unforgiving influence of many a
classical text and paths less taken. Without a doubt, every
well-rounded friar has begged for his share of texts and canons
and the such. Every act of chivalry performed of late
composed of actions derived from the verse so amiably
offered, as prerequisites necessary to graduation, by esteemed
pedagogues countrywide. There is surely no great politician
who has not, at some time enlivened behind a pulpit of the
people, recited the great words of Proust or Galileo. Yet it
remains a publicly stated fact that these great authors, along
with a slew of others, are defiled while at permanent rest by
publishers and professional appraisers at length.

I, having witnessed such atrocities committed to the
generations of poets preceding me, shall break this horrid
tradition of ethereal contempt and attempt to reap the fruits of
my labor while breath still flows from my willing lungs by
committing an atrocity of my own. At approximately 3:00
P.M., located at a position central to the Prime Meridian, I do
hereby declare the intention to put myself to death, thereby
bequeathing the worldly praise and literary worship I am due. I
shall begin offering my works at 2:00 P.M.and with each kind
tribute paid to me include a promissory note guaranteeing my
3:00 demise. All transactions occurring with due process and
haste, I have allotted myself the time period from 2:45 to 3:00
in order to bask in the Heavenly glory awarded me by
spectators and contributors alike. Although perceptions may
accumulate as to the brevity of my intended moments of bliss,
let me assure you I shall not dishonor the good names of the
aforespoken poets by kissing such a gift horse in the mouth.
My fifteen minutes of fame, no pun intended, shall be more
than one could ask for in a lifetime. Professors will be on hand
and offered the first booklets so as to immortalize me all the

more by immediately placing my works in their curriculum. I thank you now, as I will be unable to later.

97

## Sarcastic Parrot

My parrot sits,
rainbow plumage,
on the balcony rail
far above the bustle
turning a wry eye
to watch me eat my omelet.
LOOK! AWWKK! I'M A HUMAN!
His sharp beak scratches at me
Then . . .
I'M SO DRUNK! AWWKK!
His mocking beak spits at me
tottering drunkenly, slovenly
side to side
on the precipitous rail.
Another fluffy bite of chorizo
MY! BEST FRIEND! AWWKK!
His pointed beak darts up and down
SORRY MARK! AWWKK! SORRY MARK! AWWKK!
His broken record hawks at me.

The wind whips around the building's corner.

A tasty sliver of sausage
riddled with fat
slides past my tongue and gets
sideways, my eyes wide
OH GOD! AWWKK! MARK PLEASE! AWWKK!
His insinuating beak accuses as he
falls backward from the rail.
The attenuating wail becomes lost
as I hack the fatty pork
back atop my omelet.

I stare with tears at the plate
and my sarcastic parrot
alights back
on the rail.

**A Good Poem**

There's that point
in a poem
where imagery breaks down
and the words don't even know each other
and even if they did,
even if they introduced themselves
like strangers at a party
and then talked for hours
and got tipsy
and shared stories from their childhood
and then slowly established a friendship through the years
and were best friends
and one of them got married and the other one didn't
and then they grew apart as they got older
and eventually moved away from one another
and only sent letters once a year in the end,
even then
the poem wouldn't make any fucking sense.

## Uniform

the dead soldiers' Uniforms are dusty
muddy and
shrapnel bitten,
chewed by the grenade
bayonet, puncture wounded
and dyed crimson, signed in the color of a setting sun
by an unwilling author.

bloated gray bellies
distend the carefully sewn cotton
they are camouflaged
but visible just the same

i snap the picture for posterity
and think of scratch-n-sniff ads
and methane putrefaction
and wonder if a mom or dad
will point at the picture in the paper
with prideful recognition like they did when
their son of three made the post for halloween.

the family will look upon a mouth sewn shut
eyes closed
body smooth and painted
and wrapped in his sunday's best,
but I have seen the blender,
eyes wide with horror
mouth agape, twisted.
add soldiers, pulse for 20 seconds, cloths on, spread gently on
the grass.
war is not a Three Piece Suit.

# A Murder in the Woods

One day at work, I murdered a puppy with an axe.

I know that's a horrible sounding thing, but when I tell you why, I think you'll agree, you would have done the same thing.

Percy's our foreman. He's one of those people that sits in an air-conditioned truck and rides around dirt roads, up in the mountains, while the peasants like me trudge through Lewis and Clark level wilderness. Ever drive by a patch of road and see a swath of clearing disappearing over a mountain, stippled with those three-pronged power line towers? Ever wonder how those clearings stay so clear? People like me and Johnny and Red, arms and legs aching, toting our chainsaws and gas cans up and down those clearings, in 100 degree humidity.

We all get up before the ass-crack of dawn, when the roosters are still sleeping off last night, and shower and pack our lunches, before we crawl into our decades-old cars and drive 20 minutes to the meeting point - Red's house. Then the six of us sit in two rows in a dually, diesel engine humming its rhythm, and drive for 40 minutes to the hills of Ridley. The combined IQ of everybody in the truck wouldn't reach triple digits. If I sound snooty, it's because I plan to go to college one day. They can see this in me, and I can see that for them, high school was the last of their education. It's unspoken, but I get treated differently and talked to differently. You can always tell when someone's in your tribe that's not supposed to be.

It's 75 degrees and only 15 minutes past dawn when people like us are three miles deep in the woods. We start out by the river, waving our chainsaws around like Leatherface at the end of Texas Chainsaw Massacre, small branches falling on our white helmets and shoulders from above. Bugs and spiders and things that leave bites and whelps that you only feel later that night when you're finally in bed and trying, unsuccessfully, to fall asleep. We almost step on snakes at least once a week. They just lie there, waiting to the last second, like they're invisible to us if they don't move. Then they slither away and we almost shred our legs with the chainsaw trying to get away. Wasps and hornets and bumblebees and ants and mosquitoes. The list goes on.

By the end of the day, we smell like the bottom of your laundry basket. We're soaked in sweat and gasoline. If I took my shirt off and threw it against a wall, it would stick. It's Friday, so we clean and sharpen our chainsaws; a tired promise that we get to do it all again next week. If our life was a 33, it would be scratched and skipping, playing the same melancholy line over and over again.

When you're miles deep in the woods, there are no bathrooms or port-a-potties. Everybody's exhausted and ready to leave, and I have to poop. You get harassed for things like this. This part of the woods has been hit by pulp wooding, so it's open. You have to trek over a hill or hide behind a scrub of trees, squatting at an awkward angle while hanging onto a small limb, or you'll slip and shit your own pants.

When you're alone in the woods, and you hear an animal sound, it's not like hearing the same sound in your back yard. You're exposed out here. I jumped at the squeal in the distance. Then I was still and listened and there it was again. About forty feet off the main road, next to a pile of burnt junk, was a puppy. He was as helpless as I was out there. The gash on its hind quarters was wide and open. It was teeming with maggots. The poor soul was breathing heavy and slow. God knows how long it had been abandoned or what had caused that gash. And now it was being eaten by the forest from the inside out.

Like I said, when you're deep in the woods, you're exposed and vulnerable. We don't have guns on the truck. The guys aren't listening and they keep yelling about beer-thirty. Red walks back to the puppy with me. He says it's a damn shame and tells me he'll be right back. I have gas and figure it'll kill some of the maggots, so I pour it on the squirming mass, but instantly regret it. The dog starts yelping. I want to cover my ears, but don't. Red comes back with an axe. He says it's all we got. He looks like he's about to handle it, but then hands the axe to me, telling me to clean it before I put it back in the truck.

I look back on that day every now and then. I think about the differences between tribes. I reflect on what made Red hand me that axe. I believe he wanted to force me to be a member of his tribe.

I'm a senior now at our local community college. It's not much, but it'll keep me out of the deep woods, where you're exposed and vulnerable.

**Sin**

The day I dug the hole
was laborious and solemn,
unkempt hair wild in the rain
with cakey mud and deep
it went
down,
down,
down,
only a pinhole of light at the top
and then I threw in the body
and left.

I came back in ten years
gallivantin' on the baked dust plain
and there were rocks sittin' in that place
circling up a roped bucket that ran down
to the water that the people all drank
and I wondered about bacteria and death
and e. coli blackness and pissed-off cows
or whatever you call 'em
and out walked that side-of-the-road dead man
from a whirlwind tepee
still wearing that canvass suit that
married us in madness that muddy night
and pointed at me and yelled to the people
who pinched my arms and drug me to the well
where that stranger I knew
watched me enter that pinhole headfirst
to cleanse myself in the muddy wallow of Karma.

**Boxcar Shock**

Still in a box-car shock
from the train's impact,
we are twisted inside
our crumpled-up car paper

We are a Jackson Pollock

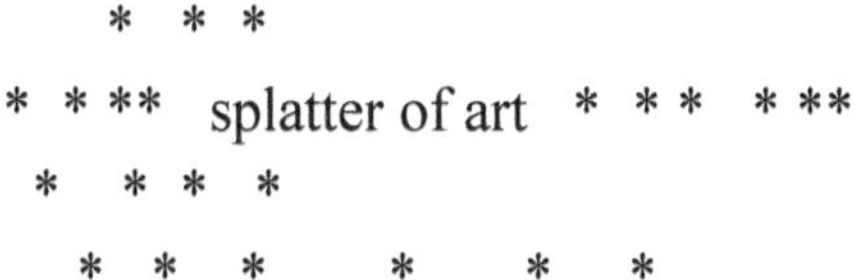


canvas raked from the smooth museum walls
and balled up like aluminum foil
until parts of us are touching other parts they shouldn't

Mother's mouth opens and closes
like a spasmodic goldfish
who is drowning for reasons unknown to it,
and amongst all that struggle
finds only one syllable - Ka

I think of Egyptian gods and cats and people with heads like
dogs

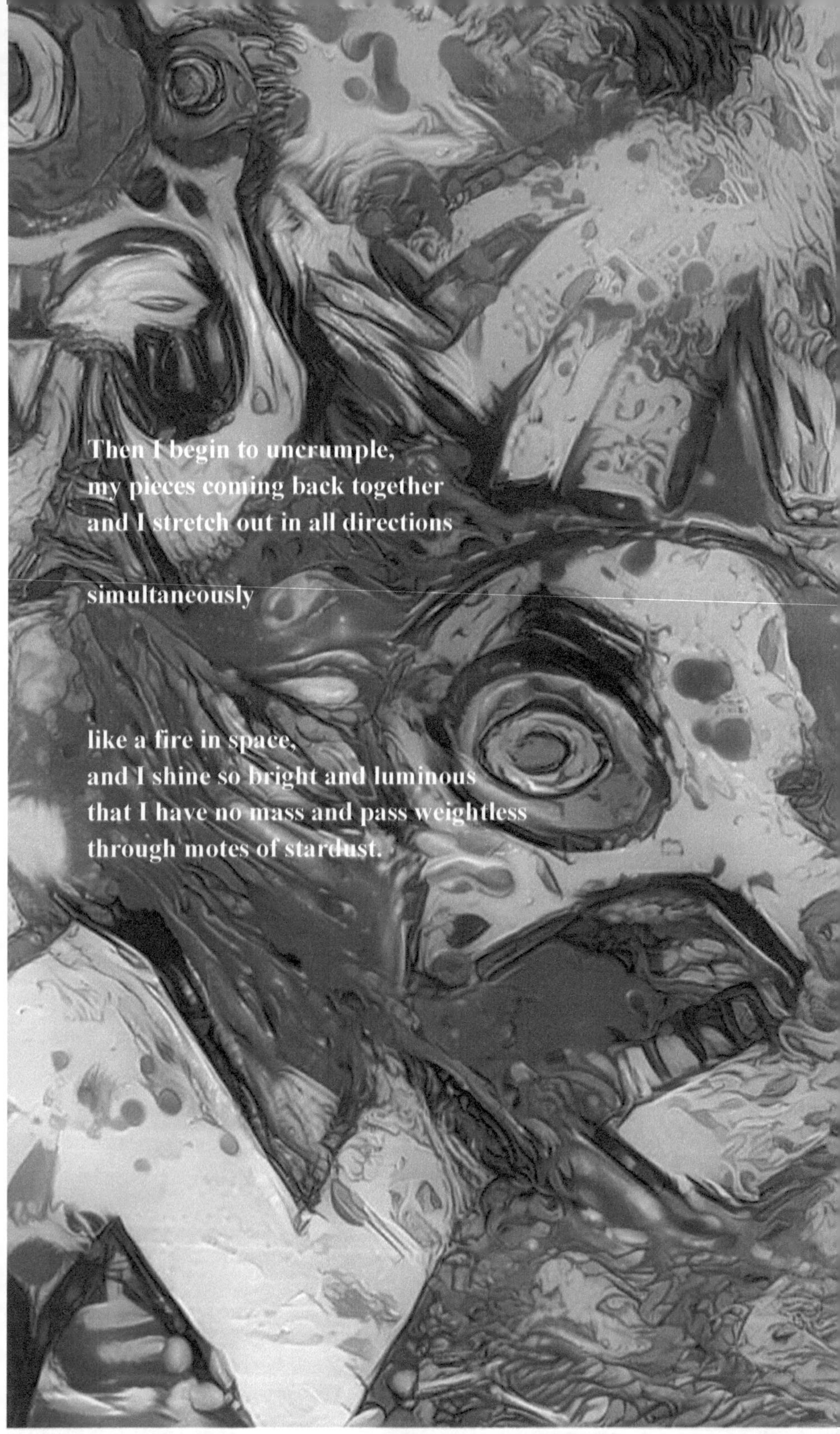
Then I begin to uncrumple,
my pieces coming back together
and I stretch out in all directions

simultaneously


like a fire in space,
and I shine so bright and luminous
that I have no mass and pass weightless
through motes of stardust.

# The Dancing Scarecrow

The scarecrow hung silent and stiff in the field of dead corn. Its hunks of stitched-together burlap pregnant with hay and infested with curious field mice. Its feet were densely packed, unopened pinecones, covered with a pair of church shoes newer than most villagers owned. They came from an out-of-town man who was hung in Rose Marie county. His pants came from a wealthy businessman who lost them in a card game. The buckle from a drunken cowboy who wondered from the path to take bodily relief one night. The shirt came from a traveling preacher who was selling fancy, gold-leafed bibles. He said the scarecrow gave him the willies, so he soaked one of his only two shirts in holy water and left it on him one hot, summer day.

One evening, when no one was around and the crows were looking the other way, the scarecrow wiggled his toes. This was a sign that he was alone. That things could be other than they were. That there was no one to take measure of things that could not be. Then he wiggled the dry husk of his fingers. Such a wonderful friction. The loud scraping filled the windless field and reverberated off the corn husks. The branches in his knees bent and snapped as he broke free of the cross he was nailed to. He looked down at his deadman's shoes and clacked his heals together, cocking his head to the side as the clicks reached his desiccated, dandelion ears. He stretched his very literal limbs to the sky, drawing up like a newborn tree in the dead rows of corn. Then he danced.

He danced a jig, the Charleston, and the Jitterbug. He reveled in the last remnants of sunshine. He put on a show for no one, executing his parts of the Waltz, Swing, and the Foxtrot with wild abandon. Straw flew this way and that; each grandiose, theatrical flourish slinging a part of him hither and thither in the field. How much time passed he did not know, for time was not present here. The only thing that existed in the here and now was a cornucopia of contentment discovered within the brazen freedom of a solitary dance. He finished dancing then bowed to no one and turned to take the path back to his cross.

Standing in front of him amid the rows of corn was a small boy, mouth agape, eyes wide. This was something that could not be. And yet it was. With some effort, the little boy turned and ran. And what does one do when something runs? We chase it! So, the scarecrow chased the little boy to the edge of the cornfield and watched him disappear into the farmhouse.

Should he follow the boy into the house? He felt not, for it was something that cannot be. There are rules you know. Perhaps not written down in a book, but they exist nonetheless. He knew this because if someone or something was around to see, he couldn't wiggle his toes. He looked down at his pinecone feet and wiggled his toes inside his nice, black shoes.

Soon, the father came out with the boy hiding behind him.

"I'll tell you what," said the father, "We'll go and see, and if he's been dancing around we'll take him to the burn pile. Deal?"

The scarecrow did not want to be burned alive, so he began running back to the cross. But no cross could be found. In his reverie, he had forgotten where the cross was. He listened for the man and boy to see where they were headed, but he couldn't tell. He ran and ran as the voices drew closer, but could not find his cross. As he threw his arms up in desperation, he saw that most of the straw inside him was gone. He had purged it while dancing. He didn't look the same as he had on the cross. He was leaner and the shirt and pants hung on him like a pirate's wet sail during a storm.

A nearby voice exclaimed, "See! See!"

The scarecrow inched closer to get a look. He could see the father and the son standing next to his cross and staring in his direction. Their eyes met. This could not be. There were rules. The scarecrow did not move any part of his body, mostly out of habit, for some time. But after a long while, he could take it no more and wiggled his pinecone toes. The boy and the man did nothing. So, the scarecrow wiggled his witch hazel fingers. The man and boy did not move. The scarecrow had a notion then and lept forward, waving his arms like a windmill. Still, the father and son did not move. He crept along the dead corn until he was a few feet from the man and child. Their eyes were wide and tears were flowing from them like a mountain spring. The scarecrow reached out and let the tears soak into the straw at his fingertips. It was warm and just and the scarecrow began to dance a little, then stopped to see if anything was out of place. If this was something that could not be. But the father and son stood motionless in the gloaming. *They* were experiencing something that could not be. The scarecrow danced and danced until the light drained from the summer sky and the father and son could only see wisps and movements from the corners of their eyes against the leaden sky.

Soon, there was a woman's voice. It carried from the house and the scarecrow ran through the brittle stalks to see. She was standing on the porch and calling out to the man and the boy. After a bit, she went inside the farmhouse and the scarecrow thought about what could be and what could not be. He wiggled his toes. Then he strolled across the yard and up the steps to the screen door. He wanted to look inside because he had never seen the inside of a house, but the lady of the house walked around the corner and stood before him in the hallway. She watched him through the screen door and did not move. They looked at each other until the woman shed tears and then the scarecrow opened the door. He felt the warmth of the house and the smell of the fireplace and remembered the burn pile the man had promised to put him in. He thought of the twigs in his arms and shoulders catching fire and how it would feel to burn. That was something that could not be. He reached up with his witch hazel fingers and let the woman's tears soak into the straw at his fingertips. It was warm and just and the scarecrow began to dance a little, then stop to see if anything was out of place. If this was something that could not be. But the woman did not move.

Then he heard voices behind him, deep in the corn. The man and the boy and the burn pile were coming. He ran out to meet them at the edge of the corn field and they stopped suddenly when they saw him. He danced over to them and they did not move. Could not move. But he was now out of sight of the house and could hear the woman screaming and running about. He danced up to the father and pulled a taut branch out of his spindly leg, then raised up the man's pantleg and feed the thin but hard branch from one ankle to the other. Blood flowed from the tiny holes, much like tears. He then repeated the process with the boy. The woman's screams filling the yard with the father and son's names. But they couldn't answer. They couldn't wiggle their toes. It was something that could not be. The scarecrow knelt and let the blood soak into the straw at his fingertips. It was warm and just and the scarecrow began to dance a little, then stopped to see if anything was out of place. If this was something that could not be.

In his enthusiasm, he did not notice the woman's screams had ceased. He stood still and listened. Scarecrows have very, very good hearing. Which makes sense because all they do is stare and listen. He could hear footsteps plodding down the dirt road. He ran through the yard and through the house and through the front door and kept running; running after the lady of the house. Because what does one instinctually do when something runs? We chase it!

Fear is a perpetual energy, and so the lady was very far ahead of the scarecrow. She had already reached the blacktop of the road into town. But that was okay, because it was a long, long way into town, and while ladies of the house eventually tire out, scarecrows never do. But then something funny happened; the scarecrow felt like he needed to stop. A light cutting through the darkness. Something was happening. Something that could not be. In the distance, a car topped the hill and headed their direction. The scarecrow tried to run back, but it was like running in molasses until the lights passed, and then he could run again. Further down the road, the woman's wails returned as she beckoned the car, and the scarecrow once more heard screaming as he ran back toward the house; shrieks from the man and boy who were now inside the house.

The scarecrow rushed inside. The man and boy slithering across the floorboards like hemorrhaging snails, a trail of blood behind them. They froze, staring up at the scarecrow with strange looks upon their faces.

Outside, the two men who had picked up the mother on the road pulled into the driveway. Fire was licking the outside of the windows. The men told the woman to stay in the car as they ran onto the porch. From the truck, the lady of the house watched as the two men stopped suddenly and did not move. The mother closed her eyes and quietly opened the driver's door of the truck and slipped out, shutting it silently behind her. She slid under the truck, never opening her eyes to get her bearings. Instead, she listened. Mothers are very, very good listeners when it comes to their children.

She heard the screen door open and slap shut. Then the splattering of thick liquid on the porch. Then footsteps coming her way, and she had to clamp her hand over her mouth so she didn't scream. The door to the truck opened and closed. Then footsteps running out into the fields. She could hear the house burning now. She waited until she couldn't stand it any longer and opened her eyes.

The lady slid out from under the truck and ran to the porch. She did not look down as she stepped over the two men on the porch. The fire was loud and covered the ceiling. She only glanced once at her husband, who was crumpled up inside the fireplace and as black as a well-seasoned, cast iron griddle. Smoke filled her lungs as she followed a trail of blood up the stairs and found her son in the hallway with his shirt wrapped around his head. He was blindly clawing his way down the hallway. She picked him up and he howled in terror until hearing her voice. She turned to go downstairs, but that small passage was the gullet of a dragon. She ran to her bedroom and they climbed onto the roof.

Flames were crawling out of all the windows and doors and the mother thought to herself that this shouldn't be happening. That this was something that could not be. Hot death was everywhere and it was a long way down. She turned, her back to the yard below, placed her child's head against her chest, and leapt backward.

***

When the firemen found the mother and child in the early morning, the child was clutching the mother in his arms and did not open his eyes until they arrived at the hospital in their sleepy, little town. When the mother healed, they moved to the city, where there was no corn and no scarecrows.

Over the years, stories spread about how people would awake from a slumber and become frozen inside their bodies, unable to move a muscle; not even wiggle their toes. Tears

115

would flow from the corners of their dilated eyes as they stared upon something that they could never recall when they woke. It was something that could not be. They would speak of something lightly scraping against their cheeks as they wept. Something that smelled of the dank earth, but was crisp and thin, like an old manuscript baked in an oven.

Doctors explained it away. A trick of the mind that cut off the body's ability to respond. But the boy who was no longer a boy knew. He knew of things that could not be. He knew if you listened hard enough, you could hear the scraping of limbs and husks as the scarecrow danced next to your bed. And if you tried hard enough, you could remember those honeysuckle eyes staring blankly into yours. And you could feel those witch hazel fingers as they soaked up your tears, warm and just.

## A Murder of Crows

I stand in the moonlight
with whispers at my back

I hold the crow in one hand
scissors in the other

We clip the wings first
with blunt force karma

Set them down in the Limestone mud
to watch them warble and scream

When they're bled and can't walk
they pale out and start to ghost

I clamp my teeth on each
individual
feather
and yank and spit
until the hairless swell is purified

We form a line
like ants in a puddle
squatting at the lake's edge
and cast our crimson pieces into the fires
just so

We follow the Scout Master
back to the tents
Our silence paid for with
full bellies.

# Practicing

Delvaggio meant to end me, but it didn't work out that way. He had me pick between three of his favorites: the marbles, the stick, and the honey.

The stick was any type of his choosing. Could be a wooden bat, a limb from a tree, or a two by four. Could be any length. And it was inserted all the way, possibly several times. I don't need to tell you where.

The honey was set on a stove and brought to boiling. He made you lie on your back and brought your feet up over your head like you was a yoga instructor or something. Then he clamped your feet to the table. They opened you up with the speculum and poured the honey in the cavity. He'd read somewhere that some cannibal tribes used this method to tenderize their meals and it stuck.

I chose the marbles 'cause they didn't go in that end. It's a huge jar though, and they don't exactly go one at a time or let you wash 'em down with a swig of whiskey or anything. They pour and shove and laugh. Thing is, I'd been preparing for a couple of years, little by little, marble by marble. Sometimes a handful. Nothing like what they did, though. Thing is, red-faced and choking and squirming, I took the whole jar.

I'd never seen Delvaggio so mad. Deal is, if you survive, you survive. They beat me a little for good measure, stripped me, and dropped me off near one of those outdoor malls. I had to walk to the hospital, three miles away, hands covering my crotch, without getting arrested and dying in some jail cell while the cops on their payroll laughed at me.

But it had been hours and my intestines had other ideas. All I could do was squat and strain. I strained so hard I thought I might pop a blood vessel. Then I heard the clatter on those outdoor tiles. It was nighttime and everyone was tipsy from barhopping, so no one was paying me attention, just keeping their distance as they moved around me. But when those shit-laden marbles started spreading out all over the walkways, the pub-crawlers started slipping and falling all over the place.

People went down like they'd been sprayed by an Uzi. That got the cops' attention. I ran in the direction of the hospital with two cops on my tail. Thing is, every few steps, I could hear the tink, tink, tink of marbles dropping behind me. The pigs ended up on the ground and I turned a corner and lost them. I made it to the hospital that night, but wasn't able to pay back Delvaggio all the money I owed by the end of that month.

So I got the honey. Funny thing is, I'm still here. I have to take food through a tube and I have one of those shit bags hanging on my wheelchair, but I'm still around. Thing is, month after that, I was still a few thousand short.

So now Delvaggio's standing in front of me with a sizeable limb from a pine tree. It's still got the bark on it and I can see some of the sap leaking out of the end where it was cut. It's about three feet long. He's not smiling like usual. Got his game face on today. Means business. Thing is, you see, I been practicing...

HOT PIZZA
CLOTHES
LINEN
SHOES

# Dementia House

*There was once a crooked house named the Never Was. It lingered in new, middle-class subdivisions and when it was done, it moved on, leaving a blank space between the non-sentient houses.*

Olivia and Ava moved into the house with their mom a month ago. Marla made the girls dinner and they sat down to eat at the table. While Olivia was telling her mom and sister about a new friend she made at school, the lights went out. It was pitch black in the house. The girls squealed and Marla announced, "Girls, calm down. I'll light a candle." But as soon as Marla scooted her chair back, the light came on.

Marla and Ava stared at Olivia's empty chair. They called her name and told her to stop playing around, but couldn't find her anywhere in the house. All the doors were locked, and the lights hadn't gone out for more than a few seconds, so she couldn't have gone far. Ava panicked and Marla threatened Olivia loudly in each room, that if she didn't come out, she would be grounded. After thirty minutes, Marla panicked too and called the neighbors, who came over and helped them look outside. Then Marla called the police, who showed up and took notes and promised to sweep the neighborhood.

Marla and Ava stayed up all night with the lights on. Sometimes they would cry together and sometimes they would scream Olivia's name throughout the house. The next day Marla called the police, but the police said they had no record of last night's incident. Marla screamed into the phone before hanging up. Then she went to the neighbors who also said they didn't remember coming over last night. They remembered Marla and Ava moving in, but didn't recall an Olivia. They asked Marla if she was okay.

Marla rushed back home and down the hall to Olivia's room. She stared at the wall where the room used to be and uttered 'No' over and over again. Ava was scared, so Marla grabbed her hand and they left the house. But then, in the car, Marla cried and explained they couldn't leave because Olivia might show up and they wouldn't be there for her. So they had to go back inside.

Ava was really scared that whatever took Olivia would get her next. So, Marla tied Ava's wrist to hers with a three-foot rope. They heated up leftovers from last night and sat at the table like they had the night before. Marla explained that if the conditions were the same as last night, Olivia might return. Ava didn't understand, but played along. They made sure to light a candle this time and set it on the table, just in case.

They were halfway through their meal when the lights went out. Ava screamed and they both stared across the table at each other's frightened faces in the candlelight. They looked at Olivia's empty chair and waited. They listened for noises in the dark, but heard nothing. Then, in the dead silence, there was a loud knock at the door. They both jumped.

Marla and Ava, bound by the rope, made their way down the hallway. Marla was in front, holding the candle. Ava didn't want to be behind her, because when she turned around the hallway disappeared into shadows and the unknown. So Marla pulled her to the front. Ava grabbed the door handle and looked back at her mom, who said, "Go ahead, baby. I'm right here." Ava turned the doorknob and the glow of the candle disappeared. There was a hollow thump on the floor behind her. Ava hollered and pulled the door open. Upon seeing her neighbor, she wrapped her arms around him, the loose rope dangling from her wrist.

"It got her! It got her, too!"

The neighbor picked her up and hugged her and told her everything would be okay. The lights came on in the house and they saw the unlit candle lying on the floor, wax splattered around it. He said they would find Marla and walked back into the house, even though Ava pleaded with him not to. He patted her head and assured her all was well. Ava told him that her mom's room wouldn't be there, but turned out it was. They looked all over the house, but couldn't find Marla. Then the neighbor said he had to put Ava down, because after five minutes she was getting heavy, even for an eight-year-old.

He sat her down in the hallway outside Marla's room. Ava was very frightened and looked down the hallway, thinking that she should run for it. Getting out of this house was the safest thing. Getting out and never coming back, ever. The neighbor was talking but he sounded further away. Ava turned to find herself alone in the hallway and the neighbor in her mom's room, turning in circles and looking confused. Then the lights went out.

Ava cried. This time, they were only out for a second. When they came back on, mom's bedroom  doorway was no longer there. Now, there was a wall. No room. Just a wall. Ava screamed and screamed and turned and ran down the hallway as fast as she could. The lights flickered, and the front door was no longer there. She turned and ran for the back door. The lights flickered on and off, on and off, on and off. There was no back door. There were no windows. She ran through the empty house, finding only hallways and walls.

She screamed for her mom and screamed for her sister until she couldn't scream anymore. She cried until there were no tears left. Then she went and sat at the kitchen table and untied the rope from her wrist. She laid it on the table and looked around the empty room. She stared into space and thought about her mom and sister. No one would remember them. She knew this. Maybe if she could remember them -

The lights went out.

******

A few weeks later, a real estate agent brought a couple of newlyweds to the house. When she brought them into the kitchen, the woman said, "I thought you said this was a new home?"

In the center of the kitchen was the only piece of furniture in the house. A round, wooden table with three chairs. On the table were a piece of rope and two plates of food. Maggots filled the plates and roaches scattered when they entered.

The agent spoke as if in a dream. "It is."

They stared at the scene for a moment that stretched far too long. Then the lights flickered and they were staring at an empty kitchen floor.

"We'll take it," they said.

# Negotiating

It was hard to keep the lawnmower running with it turned on its side. It's the push style, so I clipped the bar tight to override the safety feature, but gas kept leaking out before I could stick a hand in the blur of rotating blades. So I lugged it inside. Then I tied all four wheels with nylon and attached the cords to the four corners of my bathroom ceiling. I had to stand on the sides of the toilet to crank it. I turned up John Denver's *Country Roads* so the neighbors wouldn't get suspicious. As I crouched underneath the vibrating machine, I realized a better way to present my side of things and stood up ever so slightly. I'm not sure what happened next, but I remember a halo of blood and hair and me screaming and *mountain mama* and when I removed the duct tape from the neighbor kid's mouth he finally agreed that forty-five dollars was too much to cut my quarter of an acre yard.

## Preternatural Freelancer

Josh Pilsner awoke to the unsettling drone of a drill. What
type of drill, he could not discern through the fog that
enveloped his consciousness. His eyes slowly opened and
quickly snapped shut again. A blinding light from above
penetrated his eyelids. He was in a seated position. That much
he knew, but little else. His head was throbbing. Everything
was thick and cloudy. That horrible drill whizzing again
somewhere to his left. He tried to open his eyes once more,
and finally managed to do so, very slowly.

A woman to his left. Was he in a hospital? That smell; a
gagging mix of sterilization and death. The nurse had her back
to him, preparing something. Had he been in a wreck? What
was the last thing – Ah! He remembered now. He was at a
restaurant. Did he drink too much? Get behind the wheel? *Oh
my God! What if I hurt someone?* His neck muscles protested
with dull shards of pain as he turned his head to survey the
room. He emitted an involuntary groan as he did so. Bright
lights, a hospital bed, shelves of medical supplies, tubing
running from the wall, maybe oxygen or something, a
stainless-steel tray next to him with surgical instruments, a
very bright light stabbing him in the eyes from above, and –
wait a sec – . Surgical instruments? What the –

The nurse stood in front of him, looking down at him like a curious bystander checking on a bicyclist who's been hit by a car.

"Hey there, sweet lips," The cheery expression didn't match the tone of her voice. "Looks like I didn't give you enough anesthesia."

*Anesthesia? Surgery?*

"What happened," he mumbled. "Did I get in a wreck?"

The nurse turned to grab something, and that was when he noticed two things. One, there was a peculiar feel to his mouth, a swelling numbness and a strange vacancy of texture he felt when speaking. Two, the nurse, clad in black, had wings. He moved his tongue around some more and realized what was missing. A tooth. A front tooth at that. He pushed his tongue through the space over and over, unable to yield to the fact that one of his front teeth was no more. The nurse with dragonfly wings was holding a very large wrench. Not the kind you would use for turning a nut on a 4×4 truck, but one to turn a propeller on a cruise ship. The comically oversized kind. A strange juxtaposition between the small-framed nurse with wings and the shiny wrench that must have weighed 80 lbs.

"Sorry about that sport. I'll use a little more anesthesia this time. K?" She made an apologetic face that offered no real sympathy and then raised the huge wrench like it was a small umbrella.

Josh noticed something on her wrists and hands as she did so. Blood. He peered down at his white tank top. Blood was everywhere. He looked back up at her (and he hated to admit this, considering the circumstances) rather angelic face and saw an expression that could be considered bored amusement.

Josh whimpered, "Is that my anesthesia?"

The nurse's answer was matter of fact. "Cheapest there is. I need you to count backward from a hundred."

Josh made an attempt to block the blow. That's when he realized his hands were tied behind him.

"Ninety – . . . "

Josh Pilsner awoke to screaming. At first, he thought it was himself, but then realized he was too groggy to move, much less gather the power to shout. His head was moving back and forth and not of his own volition. The pain was unbearable. He felt like he was drowning. He gagged and struggled to breathe, but it wasn't much of a fight. His head stopped moving. There was a slurping sound as something foreign was inserted into his mouth. He managed to open his eyes in time to see the winged nurse remove what looked like a handheld vacuum cleaner. He blinked through tears. The nurse was a smeared, tangled image.

"Don't worry. It's a Dyson."

She put it back on the table. Josh already felt his mouth filling up with blood. The nurse grabbed something from his right and placed her tiny hands on his head. Her fingers clamped like a vice grip. Metal, scraping his teeth. A sickening sound. A probing, alien object in his mouth, searching, then finding purchase and a tug. A shooting pain that forced his eyes shut. Now he found the strength to scream. He stopped and for a moment was completely disoriented as the sound continued. After a few anxious seconds, he realized the screams were emanating from another room. *Another room? My God. What kind of place am I in?*

"Rere ayum eeyeh?" he garbled.

*How many teeth am I missing?*

The cute (how could he continue along that line of thought?) nurse with wings put her hands on her hips in mock exasperation. Then she picked up the wrench again.

"Your body doesn't react very well to the anesthesia."

Crimson spittle flew from his mouth as he screamed, "Ahht's behawse ihs hotah fuyeeng anehethya. Ihs a gohamn weench!"

She stared at him without saying anything for a moment. Josh had the nagging impression that accosting a 95 lb female who picked up 50 lb wrenches was not the best protocol in a situation like this. He wasn't sure what the word 'protocol' meant, but it sounded right.  While still holding the huge wrench out to her side with one hand, she uttered a question in threatening monotone.

"Do you want me to get the *really* big wrench?"

She stared at him, waiting. He stared back wide-eyed, unable to answer. He thought of what a bigger wrench might do. "No, ayam," he replied as courteously as possible.

"A tough guy, huh. No an uh steesi ah, huh."

She played with the words, mocking his inability to enunciate properly under said conditions. *No bedside manner at all*, he thought, and kept it to himself.

"Ruut appened?" he asked, red drool cascading from the corner of his mouth. He felt weak. Sluggish.

"Speed dating," she answered. "Anesthesia hasn't worn off yet, I guess. Friend introduced me to it. Definitely a quick way to get the most numbers. Best ROI."

"Awr Oh Eyah," he mumbled, silently cheering as she put down Anesthesia.

"Return on investment, duh." She gazed at him searchingly for a moment. "You're not really an investment broker, are you? I knew you were lying!" she blurted out.

"Oh arah oooh?" he countered and immediately wished he could take it back.

"Fair enough," she said, grabbing a large set of bloody pliers. His head lolled away from the sight as he grew faint. "But a girl's got to make a living, ya know?" The nurse with wings leaned in, pressing her knee into his groin to hold him in place.

"AAAAIIIIIITTTTTEE!" Josh cried. She stepped back, perturbed.

"What, Bleedy Gonzales?" She shrugged with a dainty hand on her hip, the other holding the pliers above her shoulder. She was hot in a Gothic kind of way.

"Ooh ayah ooh?" he garbled.

"Who am I? Well . . . you know what? You're not going to remember this anyway, so who cares? My name is Flora Ide. I used to work for the Preternatural Calcium Recycling Corporation. High volume. Very competitive with a commission-only salary. Do you have any idea how many people throw away their teeth when they fall out? Do you have any idea how many people don't even believe in us?" She stared at Josh, searching for some semblance of understanding.

Josh wanted to be on her side at this point. He really, really did. He shook his head in the affirmative. Satisfied, she continued.

"The only real money is in the pre-pubescent, middle-class division. But I kept getting assigned to the elderly division in Russia. Graveyard shift. Ever tried digging up a coffin that's under six feet of frozen tundra? Didn't think so. And then when you're down there, freezing your wings off (*so she does have wings*), boom! You're liable to find that grandma has an empty grill. Is 'grill' the right word nowadays?" she asked.

Josh shook his head emphatically. He *did* know what that word meant. And as long as she was talking, she wasn't pulling. His eyes were still watering. Whatever clamped his hands together behind his back was slicing into the wrist. He tried to remember how many quarts of blood were in the human body, and then attempted to compare it with the total amount on his clothes and the floor, all the while giving this nurse his full attention.

"Urah ooph aree?" he asked.

"A non-believer?" she said with disbelief. "Even after all this?" She bowed up, her shoulders swelling, and inhaling deeply, was suddenly airborne, flitting around the room with awe-inspiring speed and agility. Her wings but a blur. Then she landed in front of him hard enough to crack the concrete beneath the linoleum. She grinned ear to ear, the buzzing of her wings subsiding. There was a piercing shrill from another room.

"Anyway, there was a huge layoff a few years ago," and as she spoke, she flitted forward with no warning. He felt a jerking motion, then more blood filled his mouth. She had plucked out a tooth, by hand, in under a second. "Did you catch that? That's skill. That's professional workmanship. But they laid me off anyway. So now," she turned back to the pliers, "I'm with a group of freelancers in a small, out-of-the-way building. We're a little more proactive, but we pull in a lot more money. Say, would you like some pulp fiction to read while I continue?"

She looked serious. How could he pretend to read right now . . . to make her happy somehow, so that maybe she would . . . and then she busted out laughing.

"Get it? *Pulp* fiction?" she looked him in the eyes, askance.

Josh tried to smile, his puffy lips spreading wide over his bruised and battered face, a gaping, bloody maw dotted with a few lingering vestiges of teeth. Insecurity and fear spreading over his countenance like a tidal wave of terror.

In a dark corner of the room, where the overhead light wasn't working, Josh made out a blob where it looked like part of the ceiling had collapsed. What looked like crumbling bits of drywall was actually a humongous pile of teeth. *She said, "Out of the way place,"* he thought. Somewhere you could torture people with complete disregard for the noise, or the fact that you had wings growing out of your back. He tried to push the thought from his mind. As her knee pressed deep into his chest, he ventured one more question.

"Ere ayar ee?"

She stared at him in awkward silence. A dripping set of pliers hovering over his puppy-dog eyes, begging for mercy that would not come. She was deciding whether or not to tell him. As they were poised there, the wolf and the lamb, frozen in time, the door to the room flashed open A man stood in the doorway. A man on the top half of his body anyway. He was holding a *really* big wrench.

"Do you need this?" his guttural voice boomed, echoing like a tsunami of despair in the tiny space.

Josh answered for her.

"Yahs, peez."

SMILE

# A Murder in the Woods

I sometimes feel like there's subliminal messages everywhere I look. I guess most neurotic people would think they're only being sprinkled with foreign concepts through their TV's or the Interweb. But there's things out there most people can't see, not because they're not able, but deep down, because they don't *want* to know. These things also exist in nature, not just on the boob-tube.

That's where I'm at now. Deep in nature. Me and a crew of five other guys get dropped off at the start of one of those large swaths of power line lanes you see disappearing over a mountain as you drive by. We tote our chainsaws and gas cans for a half mile, slowly creating those open areas below the lines, all in 100-degree weather in the summer and below freezing in the winter.

I knew today was bad news. I saw a dead armadillo on the side of the road during our morning commute to the drop point. Later, I saw a bloated catfish at the river's edge. After that, it was a matter of time. Things always come in threes.

I know what you're thinking - people can see anything they want if they look long and hard enough. And that's true. But I've pointed these things out to other people, and they've seen them as well.

Truth be told, most of what I'm tuned in to are supraliminal messages, not subliminal. The difference is that subliminal means you can't actually see or hear the stimuli; that it's not something you can pick up consciously. Although, I think there are plenty of things that are subliminal that I can sense, maybe not see or hear directly, but would give me pause before they would a regular person. I'm not saying I have supernatural abilities. I'm just tuned in. I've turned the radio dial to the stations other people don't, and then I listen attentively. I respect those frequencies and they reveal themselves to me intermittently, at random times and places.

About noon, we ate our bagged lunches and lingered a bit longer than usual before starting back. It was 104 degrees and would reach 106 by three o'clock. Thirty minutes later, I was trimming a tangle of bush next to a stumpy patch on a hillside when my neck started stinging. A swarm of wasps. I ran up the hill and we all took turns throwing gas down the hill until I could recover my chainsaw. There must have been about forty or fifty wasps swarming all over, but I was only stung in three places. Like I said, things come in threes. I don't have to convince you of this. You've probably had experiences with this pattern yourself.

It is true that I've been diagnosed as schizophrenic. So, yes, I constantly hear a particular set of three people (always sets of three) whispering clues in my ear, clues about who sends the messages I receive on a daily basis. No sense in dancing around that subject. But I know what's real and what's not. I take my medicine. I talk to my shrink. I'm on level ground.

At quitting time, I had to use the bathroom. But two miles deep in the woods, there is no bathroom. So, I had to walk over a hill and roam off the road so no one could see me. When I was done, I heard a muffled squeal. I waited. Nothing. I waited a bit more, then heard it a second time, off to my left. I knew it was coming, and sure enough, a third squeal broke the silence. There, I found the most horrible thing in the world. It was a puppy, lying on its side. It had a huge gash on its hindquarters, maggots hard at work in the wound.

I know what you're thinking. Can the puppy be saved? I'm here to tell you that it could not. The wound was deep. There was an infestation. The guys I was with wouldn't have allowed it anyway. I get side-eyed enough as it is. Trying to drag a maggot-ridden, dying animal on board would have been too much for them. All that was left was to ease its misery. I returned to the truck only to find we didn't have a gun. Only an axe.

It lie on its side, head on the ground, short and shallow breath. I stood there with the axe, listening very, very hard at the puppy. There was something there at the precipice. The messages sent from that plane are the hardest to hear. Their voices faint. Their pathways to this world tenuous at best. After a couple of minutes, the puppy lifted its head and looked right at me. Its eyes were light brown. Its being was small. It was atrophied in full. I stood silent for some time, blocking out the familiar voices and listening intently for any others. Suddenly, as if it realized what I was doing, the puppy's head moved to look directly up at me a second time. Its eyes pleading. Then his head went down again. I simply couldn't do this. I would have to return to the truck and beg one of the others to follow through. It was, after all, just a puppy. And couldn't that wound be cleaned out, maybe by a vet? If I raked the maggots off and forgot about the opposition from the guys. If I took it to an emergen... But then it lifted its head a third time.

I swung the axe. It was done. But I needed to reconcile with the message, offer a destructive interference with that frequency's wavelength, so it would cancel out this channel of necessary death. I swung two more times.

Threes. It's always sets of three.

# Christmases

The horn goes off like it does every Christmas morning. Reggie calls it a Clack son. Everybody jumps out of bed like they got ants the size of rats under the covers. We don't brush our teeth Christmas morning because the horn keeps blaring until we're all downstairs in the big room. No one can even yell anything to anyone else because the horn is way louder than anyone can scream. We're all wobbly since we only got a few hours of sleep and kids bump into each other on the way out the door. Our bare feet freezing on the cold wood of the hallway floor.

We're all downstairs in less than twenty seconds. All of us stop in the middle of the big room and form a tight cluster of sleepy, little children. I hear someone say, "I don't like this part. This is just for him. Why do we have to be here?" They're talking about me. I've been trying not to think about the Christmas tree. About that corner of the room. About whether or not my truck is under there. You know what? Let me tell you about yesterday first. About Christmas Eve. Christmas Eves are the best.

# Christmas Eves

*Please God, let my brother have a really awesome Christmas wherever he is. Let him get the best gifts ever. Let him get exactly what he wants, Lord. Oh, and Mom and Dad, too. Amen.*

The sisters have us say our prayers every night, but it's Christmas Eve, so I'm saying an extra batch just for good measure. You never know.

Sister Elsie pokes her head into the doorway of our room. "Fifteen minutes until dinner, love. Wash up."

Me and Reggie get up from our game of aliens vs. army and head down the hallway to the washroom. The smell of the turkey and gravy fills every room in the small, two-story house.

Everyone is in line. We wait our turn, the cold from the hardwood floors seeping into our bare feet.

We're not supposed to, but me and Reggie wash our hands at the same time. Barkley complains that we're taking forever. Not to make fun, but Barkley is kind of fat. His belly hangs over his pants like he's a marshmallow that's melting out from under his shirt. He's been caught five or six times this past year sneaking into the kitchen at night to grab a snack. One time, him and another kid who's gone now woke up hollering. They

were covered in ants. Sister Elsie found cookies in his
pillowcase. He had bites all over his shoulder and side that
took three weeks to heal. Right now his stomach is probably
growling. Me and Reggie exchange a quick side glance and
then wash our hands for another thirty seconds.

"Guys!" he hollers.

"Enough!" comes Sister Elsie's voice from downstairs. She
can't see us, but knows something is up. One of the kids that's
gone told us one time that she had eyes in the back of her head.
We laughed and he got mad. I think he really believed that. I
couldn't say I believed him, but Sister Elsie did catch me
staring one day at the back of her neck, her black hair covered
it and so I couldn't see. "Can I help you, love?" I stammered
and stuttered and couldn't think of what to say. I didn't want to
lie, but I didn't want to tell her that I was looking to see if she
had another set of eyes under her hair. She smiled and turned
back around. A week or so after that, she was getting her hair
braided by Samantha. There were no eyes. I looked.

We sat down at the table in our assigned seats and made
steeples with our hands. "Elbows," said Sister Elsie, and Blake
and Reggie removed their elbows from the table.

*We thank you Lord for this daily bread. By your hands, we
are fed. Grant us not to jealousy, today through eternity.
Amen.*

As Sister Elsie left the room to grab the pot, I said to
Reggie, "Over the lips and past the gums, look out belly, here
it comes."

Reggie smirked. Sometimes I say things that sound
hilarious to me but that Reggie must think is stupid. Probably
it's because of the age difference. I'm ten years old and
Reggie's fifteen. I'm just happy to have him as a friend. Out of
all the other boys here, he's the most fun to play with and he
also has the biggest imagination. He says where he comes
from, you can watch TV anywhere through your glasses. He

also says you can find out anything about anything in an instant by asking your glasses. Even his Christmas wish is weird. He calls it an XBox Nitro. I've already looked stupid for believing the eyes in the neck thing, so I'm not falling for any of that. Some nights when I have trouble sleeping, Reggie will fill my mind up with his fantastical stories and I'll drift right off.

Sister Elsie brings around the tray, stopping at each person and unloading two pieces of turkey and two deviled eggs. She starts with Samantha (girls first and all that) and makes Barkley wait til last like always. We can actually hear his stomach growl this time. She returns with dressing. We're all drooling at this point. She pours the gravy. Each person gets as much as they please. Barkley's plate is a gravy soup and doesn't overflow only because Sister Elsie cuts him off after five scoops.

Sister Elsie finally says, "Dig in you little monsters." We attack the food. Forks fly into people's faces and it's amazing that no one gets impaled. No one talks. We just sit there making "Mmmhhh" sounds, mouths stuffed to the point where it's hard to chew. Barkley is done first.

Christina once spent an entire meal stealing glances at Sister Elsie, counting the number of times she chewed each bit of food. When she told us the count, we couldn't believe it. So we all tried to count for ourselves. She caught us staring and asked us what we were doing. Somebody got nervous and ratted us out. Turns out Christina was right because Sister Elsie told us herself that she chewed each bite thirty-three times! She said something about helping digestion or something. We were all quiet after that because everyone was counting how many times they were chewing their own food and then counting everyone else's chews at the table. Ever counted your own number of chews? You should sometime. Mine is right at eleven. Not swallowing something after that is really hard. At our next meal, Reggie and me had agreed to try and chew every bite of our meal thirty-three times. We gave up. Everything was mush after twenty chews.

The wait for dinner is worth it though because of the cookies. The first helping is always the best. Sister Elsie brings out the trays. There must be fifty cookies on each tray. There is a tray for every three of us. We never get to eat like this except on Christmas Eve. Don't get me wrong, they never try to starve us. Only we don't always get dessert. We shove the cookies in our mouths one after the other, the sugary icing melting quickly and forming a short-lived paste in our saliva dripping mouths. I bet nobody chewed a cookie more than three times.

Although everybody's stuffed now and just wants to go lay down in their beds we have to do the wrapping. Don't get me wrong, I don't care if other kids get more presents than us, but having to wrap them is a little bit irritating. Sister Elsie says volunteering builds character and reminds us that if people didn't volunteer their time and money then we ourselves wouldn't have any presents tomorrow morning.

We help clear the food away, wash and dry the dishes, and Sister brings out the wrapping paper and scissors and tape. She starts bringing in the gifts. It's our job to wrap them and put a number on them for the age we think they fit. And that's the first time that I think about the tree, when we start wrapping the presents. I try to put it out of my head. For now, there's plenty of light in the room.

********

Some kids like Jeffery and Reggie like wrapping other kids' gifts. I understand the point of giving so it's not a big deal. Some of the gifts I recognize and some I don't. The ones that are weird and shiny and have lots of buttons are the ones

Reggie explains to me. I wrap a Barbie, a board game I've never heard of called Dungeons and Dragons, a BB gun, a kickball, red tricycle, wooden boat, model plane, a book or two and a weird looking knife that Reggie calls a butterfly. It seems like days but it's probably only an hour before Sister Elsie rings the bell.

Sister brings out the final paper. Me and Reggie call it that because it's what we use to wrap the final and best gifts with. It's a glorious shade of purple with little designs in gold that Reggie calls flour the leash. Sister Zel brings out one super cool toy for each of us to wrap. It's not ours but we can pretend it is. Reggie says that's living precariously through someone else. When Sister Zel comes through the door with the first gift I inhale like someone threw me in a cold lake.

It's a Tonka truck! The exact one I've wanted since I was born. It's all metal so you can take it outside and fill it up with rocks and it won't dent.

She sets it down in front of Samantha. I tell her the bed can raise all the way up and that it's because of Hydraulics. She looks at me like I'm a lunatic. I add that you can put two whole concrete blocks on it. I don't know why I say that, but it rushes out. Then Sister Zel brings out the next toy and guess what? Another Tonka truck! I can feel myself getting what my parents called all jittered up. I don't even notice that I'm on my knees in the seat. The next one was a truck and so was the next one and that's when I realized that we were all getting Tonka trucks! It's my turn and Sister Zel comes through the door and I can't understand what I'm seeing.

The sister lays it down in front of me. It's yellow and the back lifts up but it's plastic. Then Sister Zel comes through the door with a full-size Tonka truck and sets it in front of Reggie who can't look at me. Sister kept bringing out trucks until everyone had a full-size truck in front of them except me. My face was hot like a frying pan. I didn't realize until I reached up to wipe a tear away that my fists were balled up so tight my fingernail was cutting into my palm. I know everyone could see me crying but I couldn't help it.

Everyone got quiet and wouldn't look my way. I grabbed the scissors and started cutting into the fancy paper. How stupid was it that some kid would get a dinky little truck wrapped in such expensive paper? Mine was smaller than the rest so it should have been easier to wrap but it took me the longest. I don't know how everyone else got theirs wrapped so perfectly so quickly. How do you even do that when it's not a box and has sharp edges? Mine was tearing a little on the top and my tears had wet the paper in one spot. I suddenly wondered what it would be like if I grabbed the scissors and...

"Are you done, Love?" asked Sister Elsie.

"Yes, Sister," my voice breaking and making me sound stupid. I was getting so mad. I thought about the Christmas tree again. Then I shoved the scissors into my left pajama pocket making sure to keep the pointy end up.

********

We wash up and brush our teeth. Samantha has blood in her mouth when she rinses and the Sisters come take her to her room. Me and Reggie see weird stuff like this all the time. It's always the same kind of thing depending on who it is. For Samantha, it's always something to do with her mouth. She either has sores or a loose tooth or bleeds at weird times. For Barkley it's food. He has some kind of tummy problems and says that he's never full no matter how much he eats. Even Reggie does this weird thing where he gets really sad or mad sometimes at night and starts hitting himself in the head or stomping one foot with the other. He never hits me though so I just try and get him to stop and if I can't then I call for a Sister.

We're all ready for bed. The quicker we get to sleep, the quicker the morning comes. The lights are turned out with only a little sliver of light through the slit in the door. We make steeples and say our prayers.

*Now I lay me down to rest, I pray the Lord my soul to test. If I should die before I wake, I pray the Lord my soul to take.*

I think about all those trucks and wonder where the kids live who will wake up tomorrow and get those perfect yellow trucks wrapped in the perfect purple and gold paper. I can feel the cold steel of the scissors against my leg and I hope I don't roll over and stick myself. I can't fall asleep.

The bell rings loud and doesn't stop. It's the worst sound in the world. We're all so tired as we stumble down the hall and sit at the table. The Sister's bring the cookie trays out and they're just as full as they were the first time. We sleepily shove them in our mouths again, one by one. I eat three before I feel sick, but I know the minimum is five. If you eat the most you get to go first in the morning. I eat my five and Reggie stops at five and a half. Barkley eats eleven. When everyone is finished we brush our teeth and go back to our rooms. My stomach feels like I swallowed glass. I'm in so much pain but I'm also very sleepy.

# Christmases

We're all standing in the middle of the big room. The foyer is well lit on three sides. One side has the fireplace that everyone huddles around during Winter. Another has the table we eat at. The stairs run up the other side. But in the far corner there are no lights. That's where the couch and Christmas tree are. We stand in the middle of the room, staring at the dark corner. You can see over there but it's like the light from the rest of the room gets dimmer and dimmer as you move towards the Christmas tree. Everything is a dull blue and you only see things in that corner when you look out of the corner of your eye.

The treetop is almost touching the ceiling and that's saying something because the foyer's ceiling is two stories tall. You can see the outline of what's on top of the tree but I don't want to think about that. No one is moving and the Sisters who normally keep us going throughout the day say nothing. They let us huddle there in the middle of the room. No one is talking. The only thing you can hear is the fire crackling.

We stand there for a very long time.

"Come now. There's presents to be opened," says Sister Elsie. I jump. It's been quiet for so long and her voice is raised like she's excited. We all move toward the couch and I think of cows and how they move together. The ones who get to the couch first mark their space because if you don't you have to sit in front of the couch on the floor, which is closer to the tree. We sit for a few minutes and let our eyes adjust. We'll have a better chance that way.

It's weird how sitting in the dark for a few minutes can help you see things better. We're all looking under the tree at the presents against the wall on the other side. I measure the distance from the bottom of the tree to the floorboards. The lower it is the harder it'll be. This Christmas it's about waist high. That's good. Lots of room to scramble.

"Barkley!" says Sister Elsie. "You ate the most cookies. You get to go first!"

Barkley doesn't move.

"Barkley," she says again but this time with an edge. Barkley moves forward slowly. When he gets to the tree he kneels down on all fours and looks to the other side, which is about the length of four of our beds because the tree is so big.

"I'm gonna be sick," he says, turning to Sister, but then we hear the branches rustling somewhere deep inside the tree and everybody inhales like they're in a cold, cold lake and Barkley is startled and knows that now is the time and he takes off like a scolded dog. We see him make it to the middle. He screams and moves wildly to the right before he reaches the other side of the tree. He's making pitiful moaning sounds as he grabs blindly at the gifts. Then he's on his way back. We can see his gift out in front of him as he slides it on the floor with one hand and scrambles madly with the other. Then something slices down through the bottom of the tree and he screams and falls. His eyes wide in the darkness. Samantha springs from the couch and dives under the tree. The things inside the tree are occupied with Barkley so now's as good a time as any. Then Reggie runs forward with another kid from the couch. I can't move.

Barkley is hurt and just lays there for a second before he starts dragging himself forward with only his arms. He's not using his legs. And then he's gone. His scream fades away like he fell off a cliff; his voice disappearing somewhere deep within the tree. Samantha screams. More of us shoot forward. I shoot forward. I think of cows again for some reason and the way their eyes can open so wide and look so amazed and scared at the same time. We're all up under the tree and scattering in zig zags like it will help. There are so many different kinds of screams. Someone's foot kicks me in the face but I don't stop and charge forward with my eyes closed. I open them and see the opposite wall right in front of me. I panic and look around to see two presents. One is a few feet ahead of me on the wall and the other is towards the center of the tree. I move to grab the present in the middle because it's closer to the way out but as I turn my head, I see something in the corner caught my attention.

The corner is the furthest from the light. It's hard to make out in the chaos but I recognize the purple and gold paper. I hear Barkley somewhere far away. I already have a present in my hand but I know that shape in the corner anywhere. I'm so scared I can't think but I let go of the smaller present and scramble into the deepest corner of darkness. Something above me makes a noise. Flapping wings. Slithering of scales. I can't tell. But I can feel the metal of the Tonka truck as my panicked hand punches through the paper and grabs a handful of the truck. I have it!

I turn to scramble out and see someone standing in front of me. I'm not sure how this person can be standing up under this waist high Christmas tree. I freeze in place, my hand tightening on the yellow Tonka at my side. I know I should juke to the right and make for it but I can't bring myself to do it. I am perfectly motionless for a full minute which is an eternity under this tree. My eyes start to slowly make out what's in front of me.

The reason it's able to stand up under the tree is because it's only four years old. It's my brother. His name is Marcus.


********


We woke up like always and went in our mom and dad's room and jumped on the bed and pestered them until they were awake. This Christmas was different because Marcus could finally understand what was going on this year. The end of the hall was always awesome because when you reached it you could see into the living room. Santa's presents were always front and center.

This was good year because we both had tons of gifts under the tree. But as we ran to the gifts I could tell something was wrong. Mine was really small and his was really big. And when he tore that purple and gold paper off that Tonka truck, I couldn't believe that Santa had done that. I'd been so good that year. Marcus was still pooping in his pants. I opened mine and it was a truck, but small and plastic. I looked to mom who was giving dad some kind of look and I said, "That's mine!"

Marcus screamed that it wasn't and when Marcus looked away mom made the shush sign to me like I was in the library or something. She told me to wait just a second and pulled dad into the other room. I got all jittered up I guess because the next thing I know I had jerked the truck from Marcus's hands and when I did he fell over and then I was hitting him with the Tonka truck over and over until I flew up in the air. Dad grabbed me so hard that the Tonka flew out of my hands and skidded under the Christmas tree. I was shouting and dad was yelling and mom was shrieking. Then dad said *What?* and I fell on the floor really hard. They were holding Marcus like he was a doll and he was all limp and mom started wailing like a banshee and saying *No* so many times and dad picked me up and screamed the word *Why* so many times and then he was shaking me and I heard mom call his name and then I woke up here with the Sisters.

I'm always under the tree when I remember what happened and how many Christmases I've had here. Marcus grabs me and drags me though the harsh bramble, deeper into the tree. The branches and needles stab and scrape. Some places are so thick with prickly branches I don't think he can drag me any further, but he does anyway. I'm screaming and crying for all the good that'll do. We get to the deep of the tree and my hands are pulled above me and tied with barbed wire tinsel. My shirt is pulled up to expose my belly. It's scratched and bloody and that's when I hear Barkley slithering through the branches.

"I'm sooooo huuuuungry," he whispers. "Soooo, soooo hungry."

Marcus slides his hand in my pocket and pulls out the scissors I was going to use to protect myself. His tiny, bruised hands start sliding the scissors under the skin at my belly button like I was the wrapping paper. I can't see what's happening, but I can feel Barkley gnawing into my belly to get at the cookies. Barkley's head is inside me now.

My brother is there in front of me in the blue darkness. His face is pale and his eyes are wide. Even though it doesn't make sense, I truly believe this is my brother Marcus.

And as I scream and scream and scream into the never-ending branches, I think of the Tonka truck somewhere below.

## How to Properly Dispose of Dead Children

**Step 1:** Poke 'em. Make sure those little boogers are caput. Nothing is worse than waking up to a bloody trail out the front door. Although the manual offers several "scientific" methods, the time-tested method involves only a stick. There's no need to be shy. Although it should be said that jamming a wooden spear into, say, the eye socket for instance, will not yield the desired results. There is simply no way to measure the blink reflex if the blinker has been detached.

**Step 2:** Kodak moments. Capture the moment. Sometimes the overwhelming need to kill pops up at the most inconvenient times. Say you're at a neighbor kid's birthday party and everyone is yelling and screaming and not minding and complaining and you get that urge to, let's just say, end the party prematurely. A way to not lose focus is to pull out a Kodak moment from the past. Reliving the good ole times can inject a snapshot of nostalgia into the moment and stave off those silly compulsions. Remember that Polaroid hard copies are your friend. The cloud is not. It might be easier to pull up Little Johnny on Google Photos, but colleagues at work tend to frown on those accidental email attachments that you mislabeled for obfuscation purposes. And don't spend all your time wrestling with rigor mortis to get that perfect shot. A pair of good scissors will remove the lips in a jiff, leaving the perfect smile every time.

**Step 3:** Evacuation. This is the whole 80/20 rule. Spend your time on the front end and save time dealing with their back end. A slow, dreadful build, followed by a thorough terrorizing, will lead to evacuation of the bowels. Constipation is your enemy, so stay away from fat kids who eat a lot of cheese. If a few fishhooks or a little drilling doesn't do the job, try a couple of chili dogs and coffee. Works wonders.

**Step 4:** Cooking out. We all want to fire up the grill during the Summertime, but one should be sensitive to the fact that each little person has their own pungent aroma, one that may not tickle the fancy of nosy neighbors. Regardless of what the manual says, no amount of BBQ sauce can mask this. Remember not to skimp on size when purchasing a cooker. A smaller barbecue will necessitate disassembly to fit all body parts on the grill, which will require more time and tools. Plus, overcrowding the grill can lead to uneven browning and soggy areas. Don't let a few hundred dollars rob you of a crispy outer layer.

**Step 5:** Sharing is caring. You can't keep evidence hanging around and you can't eat it all yourself. You know you can't. So, sharing that BBQ is an important step in letting go. The average Joe's palate isn't refined enough to appreciate the long pig, so you'll have to add some store-bought filler. Brisket is best. Any questions from those picky eaters, say, Little Johnny's mom or pop for instance, can be assuaged by prefixing the word "brisket" with the name of a South American country. The middle class never investigate their own ignorance when challenged with an unknown word or delicacy, like say, Peruvian Brisket. A glib "Oh, okay" and the dinner party can move on.

**Step 6:** Relax. Look at the good job you've done (it's more of a calling than a job though, am I right?). You deserve pampering. After a little self-flagellation and listening to the police scanner, it's time for that trip to the skating rink. Make sure to leave by eight though so you can get home and write that Sunday sermon.

*Page left unintentionally blank*

## Author's Notes

I didn't want to put this here. I mean, what's wrong with a little vagueness in your life? Not everything should be as clean and trimmed as your mom. But then I started thinking about all those poems I was forced to read in High School and College.

**Firefly** – When I was a little shit, I used to stand in our backyard at dusk and swat lightening bugs with my yellow, Wiffle bat. If I timed it right, there would be a neon smear on the bat. I was ruthless and my goal was to have a bat that glowed like a light saber before I had to go inside.

**High Tide** – I can't think about anyone being buried in sand at the beach without thinking about the 1982 *Creepshow* movie. When you're having fun, it's never time to go. So, what if you didn't have to?

**Stereotypes** – We approach stereotypes in such awkward ways. This is a person who has stereotyped an insect to the point where he's so uptight, he can't communicate with it.

**The Last Anything** – We don't trust the last of anything on the store shelves. I think we're like this sometimes with people.

**Fishing With Walter** – Fun poem about a random event that causes an aversion to flying.

**Nurture** – A farmer's wife has obviously got on his last nerve, so he fixes that once and for all. Then pretends to follow her instructions for life to the letter as he moves through his days.

**Scientific Inertia** – A guy once told me all those black holes in the universe were civilizations that had found the God particle. It could be anything that we don't fully understand, but poke with that scientific stick anyway. When the atomic bomb was being constructed, some people were afraid the atoms would keep splitting and it would destroy everything. In this case, gravity reverses itself.

**Things Could be Worse** – This would seriously change the way we live. Mosquitoes are the closest, similar thing here, but they let go after latching on. Ticks burrow into your skin and stay there. Pull them out wrong? They'll cause disease.

**Shiny Happy People** – If you were made of something reflective, narcissists would stare at you, so they could see themselves. Others would stay away. Most people do not want to constantly reflect on who they really are. A little reflection is good, but a lot can lead to issues.

**Board and Nails** – Kids these days, ammarite?

**Ego** – Us poets do what we think is cool. Poet cool. And then the Normals pat us on the shoulder and tell us they'll put our works on the refrigerator. Good job, buddy!

**Dancing Scarecrows** – Who knows what these bastards do when we're not looking?

**The Clock** – We're individualistic materialists. We shouldn't be. We know this.

**Cupid's Rusted** – I'm not sure we can pass over to a Utopian afterlife and carry the painful loss of love with us. Cupid is catching this lovely, viscous venom to dip his arrows in. Little shit.

**Green Thumb** – Because everything she plants, sprouts up. Come on man, stay with me.

**ELO** – Who hasn't been sucked into a black hole, ammarite?

**Behavioral Psychology of Woodpeckers** – Sometimes it seems like things come to people easier than it does for us. And when we try to repeat what those lucky bastards are doing, we never get the same results. We get the short end of the stick.

**Changing Stations** – This is based on a true story. If that guy in the car next to us wouldn't have been fucking with his radio, me or the wife may not be here now. I have no idea if the guy pulled through or not. Hope he's alright. If I sound classist or overly irritated with the two women who caused the wreck, it's because, at least in the moment, they didn't seem empathetic to their victim's plight. If I had almost killed a man because of my stupidity, and I was okay, I would be over there helping.

**Unspoken** – We don't always say what we wish we could to the people we love. Maybe it would sound too stupid or awkward or like we were quoting some movie. And then those people die. And we feel like shit. But what if they got a book when they reached the other side? One that was full of what you meant to say, but didn't.

**Life Is** – If you strip away the fancy stuff, you get at the heart of things. So what if you stripped away almost everything? What would matter? Each section after the first explores what would happen in different situations. You're alone. You're alone, but with a toy. You have someone to spend the time with. You're a have. You're a have not. And the last, repeating stanza is an open invitation that says, "So, what do you think matters?"

**Buttercream** – This might be recycled, but that's okay. Guy comes home and gets locked in because he's a werewolf, but his friends are locked in with him.

**Preposthumous Poet** – The only way to be a famous poet is to have been dead for some time. And then, if you're lucky, you go viral for some random reason and others get rich from reprints. This is me short circuiting the process and killing myself at a predetermined time.

**Sarcastic Parrot** – The parrot saw what happened. It knows.

**A Good Poem** – When it comes to poetic talent, just making it rain…

**Will Power** – Two people are worried about this man's will power, but for different reasons.

**Uniform** – You sign up for some jobs and you're romanticized as a hero with no prerequisites. But you can be in the military or a fireman or a policeman and be a huge asshole who never comes close to doing anything heroic. Not taking away from people who are willing to risk their lives for strangers, but that uniform itself doesn't mean shit. It's the person inside it. And when your son or daughter or mother or father comes home in a body bag, all that thank-you-for-your-service stuff doesn't mean shit. Let's stop romanticizing war and making videos where someone getting to come home after six months because they're not dead is fodder for some good feels. Because for every one of those that makes it, someone else gets a coffin.

**Sin** – A random act of hate and murder are paid for years later in a mysterious manner.

**Baptist Outpatient** – What if you could have your religion removed via outpatient surgery? What would the prep work look like? I'm not saying all Christians are bad, but I do see why sometimes they were thrown to the lions.

**Boxcar Shock** – A train crashes into a family's car. This is from the point of view of a child in the wreck who is passing on.

**The Dancing Scarecrow** – Scarecrows don't come to life, dance around, and try to kill you. That is something that *cannot be*. But what if scarecrows *can* do whatever they want until we observe them? Only then, are they unable to move. Perhaps they see this as normal, like we do from our side. But what if those roles were reversed?

**A Murder of Crows** – This has a *Hereditary* feel, with the clippers and all, but with Boy Scouts. Who knows what these people do in the woods?

**Practicing** – I was in a Chuck Palahniuk mood when I wrote this. Not sure if I channeled him correctly, but that's how it felt.

**The Sixth Course** – Serial killers have awkward first dates, too.

**Dementia House** – What if there was a house that had dementia, and when it forgot about you, you were simply no more?

**Negotiating** – Kids want a lot of money to cut your yard nowadays. That's all I'm saying.

**Cold Pasta** – Some cops ask a cannibalistic serial killer how dead skin tastes and he gives them an all too realistic description. This comes from me eating a piece of cold macaroni that didn't have any cheese on it. Don't believe me? Try it. Fucking disgusting.

**Preternatural Freelancer** – A man realizes that he's in the tooth fairy's hell den.

**A Murder in the Woods** – Unfortunately, based on a true story. This happened in my early 20's when I worked for a tree crew. As I explored my mercy killing later in life, I thought about how people might take it based on how I relayed the experience on paper. It turned into three short stories written in the same style as Yan Martel's letters from the warden stories in *The Facts Behind the Helsinki Roccamatios*. Of course, his has more subtle changes and is a much better exploration of how these tiny changes can make big differences. Think what I did was horrible? What would you have done?

**Illustrators**

**Sebastian Mateo Cardo**
*Stereotypes*
*Dingle Tree*
My name is Mateo Cardo (Mateoscopio). I have been drawing and painting since a child, using mainly watercolor, ink, and acrylic. I abandoned my profession as a lawyer for many years and devoted myself fully to art. Now, I work as a freelance illustrator and concept artist.
https://mateoscopio.com/
Instagram: @mateoscopio

**Russel Helix**
*Nurture*
*Boxcar Shock*
*Spiders in the Bed* (Front Cover)
An extra-terrestrial sent here on Earth to observe, illustrate, and probe. . .in no particular order.
https://www.behance.net/russellhelix
https://www.instagram.com/russel_helix

**Chinmayee Sathish**
*Sin*

**Edward Trulook**
*Baptist Outpatient*
*Preternatual Freelancer*
Hi, I'm Edward Trulook, I love pizza and drawing manga. This job has been a lot of fun, and I hope you like it as much as I do. You can follow me on Facebook as Edward Trulooks or Instagram as @edward_trulooks

## Intan Zulkifli
*Firefly*
*High Tide*
*Board and Nails*
Intan Zulkifli is currently a sophomore at the Milwaukee Institute of Art & Design. She specializes in character/world design and development with a passion for storytelling in illustrated media. You can find more of her work on Instagram: @sugargrimm, or in her portfolio on Behance.

## Vince Fernandez
*Cold Pasta*
Vince Fernandez (@dead_cvlt) is a visual artist that dips his hand onto everything "dark". His artworks depict the macabre and spook that some refuse to tread. He currently works as a freelance artist and a tattooist.
https://www.instagram.com/dead_cvlt
https://www.behance.net/dead_cvlt
https://www.artstation.com.vincefernandez3

## Eva Bailey
*Things Could be Worse*
Eva is a retired environmental consultant. She has dabbled in art and photography her whole life.

## Natalya Chizhova
*Practicing*

## Bethany Robertson
*Headless Horseman*

**Yulia Chukova**
*Negotiating*

**Anastasiya Belaichuk**
*The Dancing Scarecrow*
*A Murder of Crows*

**Anna Katorhina**
*The Dancing Scarecrow*
*Christmases* (Back Cover)
*Cupid's Rusted*
ArtStation link: https://www.artstation.com/annakatorhina

**Victoria Akinkunmi**
*Cover design*
Victoria Akinkunmi has been creating book covers and interior layouts for over 3 years. Outside of work, she enjoys long walks and good books. You can reach her on Twitter @vikky_akin or va.akinkunmi@gmail.com

**Woodcutter Manero**
Front cover font GRAPHIC PSYCHOPATHY
www.woodcutter.es

**E.M. Kinga Mac**
A dedicated (and very appreciated) editor. Any errors you see are intentional on my part, usually for colloquial purposes.
editingkinga@gmail.com

**Shawn Bailey**
https://linktr.ee/shawndotbailey

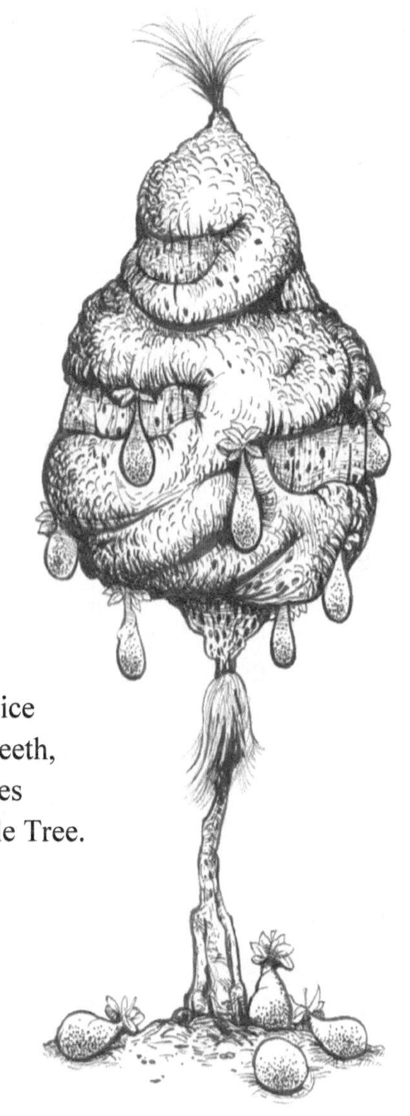

A piece of advice
to keep clean teeth,
never eat berries
from the Dingle Tree.

# Acknowledgements

I owe an immense gratitude to all of the illustrators. Please take a minute to visit their sites and check out their other artworks. This vanity project wouldn't be the same without their amazing contributions. I am forever indebted to them all.

A special shout out to Anna Katorhina, a Ukrainian artist who has been uprooted during the war. When I found out she was okay and asked if she needed anything, Anna simply wanted me to approve her initial sketch so she could start on the final illustration. *Cupid's Rusted* is one of the most beautiful artworks in the book. I wish you and your countrymen well.

This collection started because of my grandmother, Ella Bailey. She was an avid reader and had some poems published in a 1941 book. I've had the book in my possession for some time, and love flipping to the poems every now and then to touch a part of the past with which I have some commonality. As it turns out, my aunt asked about the book and we learned there was only one other copy online for sale. Just two books away from us never being able to read her work. I always wondered if MawMaw had written other things, and found out she had indeed written a children's book that has been lost to time. I put together this subset of poems so my great grandchildren could easily find my works if they were inclined. So, thanks MawMaw for submitting your work 80 years ago so I can touch your words today.

STOP